"Compelling, spunky, and instantly likable. From the UK to Japan and back, Hugh Ashton's Leo's Luck delivers a high-tension blend of behind-the-scenes rock 'n' roll, high-tech capers, and yakuza thugs."

Barry Lancet, award-winning author of JAPANTOWN and TOKYO KILL

"Leo's Luck reads like Richard Parker (Donald Westlake) crossed with Murakami – the witty tone and hard-boiled Tokyo go together like deep fried sushi. If you think that's unappetizing you've never tried the good stuff. Improbably plausible with a sci-fi twist to keep you on your toes, casual violence, and dark humor. Ashton captures the subtleties and strangeness of Japan's megalopolis as only a long-term veteran could."

Jake Adelstein, author of *Tokyo Vice*, soon to be a movie starring Daniel Radcliffe

"Hugh Ashton steps out of his usual wheelhouse with this book, but you'd never know it as he handles an unfamiliar world with the depth and skill of a master craftsman. A wonderful mix of character and originality."

Percival Constantine, author of the pulp action/adventure series *The Myth Hunter*

Leo's Luck

Leo's Luck

Hugh Ashton
Published by j-views Publishing, 2018
© 2016, 2018 Hugh Ashton
ISBN-13: 978-1-912605-33-0
ISBN-10: 1-91-260533-3

This is a work of fiction. Names, characters, places, brands, media, and incidents are the product of the author's imagination.

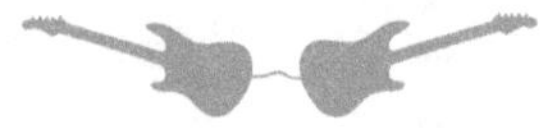

Dedication

To all those with whom I have shared the joy of creating and performing music.

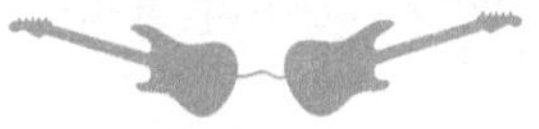

Acknowledgments

Thanks are due to many people, from many different walks of life, who have inspired and facilitated this story.

To Yoshiko, who has had to put up with a temperamental writer, whose emotions have not always been predictable or easy to live with.

To all those who have gone further than me in the musical life, thereby educating me in the highways and byways of this strange world.

To the members of the Cambridge University Society for Psychical Research, and many others in the field, who kindled my interest in the subject.

To those, notably Andy Boerger, who took the trouble to read early drafts of the novel and suggest improvements, without whom the ending would be much less than it is now. And because I promised her that she would get a mention, thanks to my Facebook friend Nazish Ahmad, who came up with the phrase "bless your peachy little heart", which I liked so much that I borrowed it (with her permission) to be spoken by one of the characters in this story.

To the readers of my other books, who have conspired to persuade me that I do indeed write things that others want to read.

And lastly, but by no means least, the staff of Inknbeans Press, especially Jo, without whose constant support and encouragement, provided generously and unstintingly despite a plethora of her own personal issues, this book would never have seen the light of day.

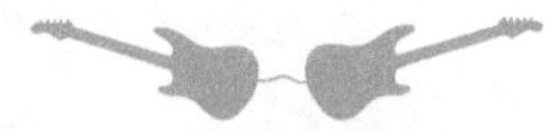

Leo's Luck

Hugh Ashton

J-Views Publishing

Lichfield, UK

"**I** don't think you understood me," said Leo. "I didn't say I wanted a separation. I said I wanted a divorce."

The last word hung in the air between him and Gail like a small purple bubble of poison gas. She waved her hand in front of her face, as if she could actually see the bubble, and batted it away.

"Well," Gail said, and shrugged her shoulders. "If that's what you want, that's what you're going to get, I guess. Don't you always get what you want? When it's time to eat out, don't we always eat where you choose for us to eat? We turn on the TV, and don't we always watch the programmes you want to watch? I can't remember the last time we went out and saw a film that I wanted to see. So if it's a divorce you want, then that's what you'll get, I guess."

He sat there, seemingly stunned by what he had just heard. "Aren't you even going to ask me who she is?" he demanded. "Aren't you even curious?"

"Oh, it's a she, is it?" she sneered. "From the attention you've paid to me in bed these past months, I thought it might be a he. Actually, I don't need to ask. It's that skinny blonde with the long legs who works Wednesday nights down at the video rental place, isn't it?"

"How did you...?"

"I think you might credit me with a little intelligence now and again. I am sure she picked out the really juicy titles from those back shelves marked 'Adults only', and you and she went back to her poky little flat in Willow Grove and watched them before the two of you played whatever nasty little games you'd just watched on the screen. No wonder you're not interested in me. I don't turn you on with that stuff beforehand, do I?"

"She is not skinny. She's thinner than you, anyway."

"And tits like a couple of half lemons, I bet."

"Not lemons," he said. "Decent-sized oranges at least..." He stopped. Gail was laughing.

"Decent-sized oranges?" she giggled. "Not even grapefruit?"

"Damn you!" He stood up, the whole six foot three beanpole of him, his head almost brushing the ceiling of the small kitchen, and pushed his chair back. It fell over, frightening the cat, already unnerved by the almost palpable tension in the room, and which leaped, screeching, into Gail's lap.

"You frightened the cat," she said to him.

"Always stating the bloody obvious." He stormed out of the room, pulled on his coat, and walked out of the house, slamming the door behind him.

It was raining. It was always raining in this bloody town. Why had they chosen to live in such a shitty place? Because of his job, he said to himself. That's why. The job he'd chosen for himself and didn't have any more. And the poky little house he now hated so much that he felt almost physically sick every time he walked through the front door? That was his choice as well. She'd wanted the larger semi-detached out of the centre of the town, but he'd argued that it was too much for them to take care of, the garden was too big for them, and anyway, it was too far to walk to the shops. So he couldn't blame her for where he was living.

Bloody woman, he thought to himself. Always tired, always complaining about him being in the house, never doing the bloody housework. Mess and dirt everywhere. She never picked up his books or washed out his beer glasses or anything. And her cooking tasted like shit. Always trying to make him eat what she called "healthy" food, that looked and tasted like sawdust. She looked at a plate of egg and chips as though it was something the cat had sicked up. And the bloody cat. Don't get him started on the way that she petted and cuddled that damn animal...

He walked on, head down, swearing moodily to himself, and so engrossed in his own thoughts that he didn't notice the other pedestrians looking at his moving lips and giving him a wide berth, looks of deep suspicion on their faces. After about ten minutes, he found he had run out of obscenities and was repeating himself, and looked up to see where he was. Oh, Christ! His feet had carried him to Willow Grove without his having been aware of it.

Leo looked at his watch. Too early to call on Sharon? No, she'd be pleased to see him. A morning quickie would put him in a better mood, and would set her up for the day, too.

He climbed the familiar staircase and knocked on the door.

"Oh shit," came a familiar voice through the door. "If

you're the papers, I'll pay you next week. I don't have the cash on me right now."

"It's Leo," he called.

"I can't talk to you now," she answered him through the closed door.

"You are talking to me," he pointed out.

"I mean, you can't come in." The door opened to reveal a tall blonde carelessly wrapped in a white towelling bathrobe, which flopped open, showing a pink nipple. She is skinny, Gail is right, he thought, as if seeing her for the first time. And she does have small tits. But her legs are long, though. And he wanted her.

"What the hell do you want at this time of the morning?" All five foot ten of her seemed to be quivering, but he couldn't tell whether it was with fear or anger. As he opened his mouth to argue, a male voice came from the bedroom.

"Who is it, Shar? Do you want me to come and tell him to fuck off?" The voice was a lazy drawl, not like Sharon's clipped urban accent.

"I'm just going," Leo shouted back at the bedroom. "You won't even have to get out of bed." His stomach was churning, and he felt sick as he watched Sharon close the door in his face.

"And you needn't bother coming round on Friday night," she shouted through the door. "I'm going to have some fun for a change."

So what was it they'd been doing if it wasn't fun? he asked himself bitterly, as he shambled down the stairs. He hadn't had the heart to argue back. If you'd been a real man, a small part of him told another part of himself, you would have marched into the bedroom, hauled the little squirt out of the bed, kicked his arse for him, and shoved him out into the hallway without his clothes. And then it would have been time to deal with Sharon...

But he knew that was a fantasy way beyond his capabilities. Leo had never been a fighter, and the idea of physical pain (his own, that is) repelled him. He would no more walk into Sharon's bedroom and tackle the unknown opponent (who might not, after all, be a little squirt, but a top-flight rugger player) than he would leap out of the window and attempt to fly.

He felt in his pockets, and came up with a few pound coins and a handful of miscellaneous silver and copper. He patted his other pockets, but failed to discover his wallet. If he were to go back home now, Gail would just laugh at him. She could tell he'd been to see Sharon, and she would know exactly what had gone on. God knows how she would know, but she would. Women had this instinct about these things.

But if he didn't go back, what might happen? She might cut up all his credit cards, after cleaning out all the cash. Or even worse, she might use the credit cards, firing up the computer, and ordering piles of stuff from Amazon. And then the bills would arrive, and they'd take months, if not years, to pay off. Could you still be put in prison for debt? He wasn't sure, but he wouldn't be surprised if it was possible.

He turned back and walked towards his house. His house? Their house. The deeds were in his name and Gail's. So if there was going to be a divorce, something would have to be done about that. Lawyers. More money that he didn't have. Shit.

And suppose he changed his mind about a divorce, and told Gail that he wanted to stay with her? Would she forgive him? Well, of course she would. I mean, she'd married him for better or for worse, hadn't she?

Well, even if this was one of the worse times, she'd stick with him. Wouldn't she?

A cold sweat covered his face, and the blender started up inside his guts again. He stopped in the middle of the street, put his hands over his face and moaned softly.

"Come on, mate," said a voice as a hand patted his shoulder. "It's not that bad, is it? I've come down off the shitty stuff a few times, and I'm still alive."

"It's nothing like that," said Leo, taking his hands from his face, and looking at the speaker, who was dressed in a biker's leather jacket and scruffy black T-shirt with filthy jeans. The face was framed in a mane of greasy black hair, tied in a clumsy ponytail at the back. The hand that wasn't on Leo's shoulder was holding a guitar case.

Leo looked at the case. "Gibson 335?" he asked.

The other nodded. "Close. A 330. How d'you work it out?"

"It's not an acoustic and it's too big for a Les Paul or an SG. Doesn't look like a Firebird. And what else is it going to be with a Gibson badge on it?"

"Smart. Know something about guitars, then?"

"A bit."

"Play?"

"Not really. Just a bit. A few chords." He looked more closely at the other and started back with a jerk. "Jesus Christ! You're Nick Lakone, aren't you? From the Killer Rabbits?"

"So? I'm not ashamed of it. I don't shout about it, either. You want my autograph? It looks like what you need is a nice cup of tea, mate, not an autograph." Despite the biker look, he sounded more like Leo's grandmother. "Come on. You can tell me what's up while we have a cuppa together. I'm good at listening to other people, I am. One of my talents. When we're on the road, my door's always open. The other guys in the band, the roadies, whoever. Even the groupies come and tell me their troubles."

"Is that before or after you fuck their brains out?" Leo sneered. The man was obviously trying to be friendly. Trying too hard, Leo told himself. But what did he have to offer a rock star? Not money, to be sure.

"I suppose I should hit you in the teeth for saying that," said Nick. "But I won't, for two reasons. First off, we've got a gig tonight and I don't want to do my hands in. Second, you're in a bad way, and I don't think you know what you're saying, or who you're saying it to. So let's go and get that tea." He grabbed Leo's arm in a way that left Leo no choice but to come along. "Oh, and by the way, I don't fuck groupies. I wouldn't want to catch anything from the other guys who've fucked them. Paul's going to be dead from AIDS in a few years. I reckon Bobby's got syphilis. Leo's got— What's up?"

"That's my name. Leo."

"Pleased to meet you. Leo what?" Leo remained silent. "You'll tell me or you won't. Doesn't matter that much to me right now. Might later. Here we are." He talked in quick disjointed bursts, as if a battery inside him was running down, and only providing sudden spasmodic bursts of energy to power him. He ignored the Starbucks in the High Street and entered the café next door to the green and white invader, where he was obviously known by the owner.

"How's it going, Nick? And who's your friend?"

"Could be worse, Ernie. This is little lost Leo. Two teas, if you would."

Leo was irritated by this casual description of himself, but held his peace. He had to admit that it was a reasonable way to refer to him at the moment, though.

"You need the sugar," Nick said when the teas arrived, shovelling three heaped spoonfuls into Leo's mug.

"I don't take sugar," Leo protested.

"Dieting? Diabetic?" Leo shook his head. "Then bugger that. You're taking sugar now, because I say so. Okay?" There was a quiet authority in Nick's voice.

The tea was hot, milky, sweet and very good. It was very different from the special Darjeeling mixed with Lapsang Souchong that Leo insisted they drank at home – what and where was home now? – but it was what he needed right now.

"So?" Nick invited when the mugs were half-empty. "It's not drink, or I'd have smelled it. You tell me it's not the other, and I believe you. So it's a woman?"

Leo shook his head.

"Okay, so you're gay. I'm not that way myself, but I don't give a shit if someone else is. So tell me all."

In spite of himself, Leo smiled. "No, it's not a woman. It's two women."

Nick grinned, displaying a set of uneven yellowing teeth. "Sounds like a good story. So tell it."

Chapter 2

"So you're tired of your wife?" said Nick, two mugs of tea later. "Happens to a lot of us. Happened to me once."

"Didn't know you'd been married," said Leo.

"Haven't. Good as married, though. Still am."

"Same one?"

"Yes." He took a pull at his tea. "Forget the little bit on the side, mate. She sounds like the sort of tart that's nothing but trouble."

"She told me she'd marry me if I divorced Gail," Leo protested.

Nick laughed. "They do that, some of them, don't they? What did she take off you?"

"She didn't. She's not that sort." Leo bristled.

"OK, mate, keep your hair on. Let me put it another way. What did you give her for her birthday?"

"New flat-screen TV."

"And for Christmas?"

"A diamond ring. We thought it was a sort of engagement ring."

"Seen her wearing it since then?"

"A couple of times. Not recently. She said it was too flashy for everyday. Oh, Jesus, you don't think she—?"

"You a gambling man, Leo? No, I won't take your money on that one. And I'm not going to make another bet with you. You couldn't afford the TV or the ring, and you've been worried sick that your missus is going to ask where the money's gone?" Leo nodded. "See, I told you I was good with people, didn't I?"

"All right, damn you. Stop being so bloody clever, and tell me what I am going to do."

Nick finished his tea. "There's something else you're not telling me, isn't there? I know it."

Leo looked around the room. They were the only people in the café. Ernie, the owner, had gone behind the counter and seemed to be busy counting saucers or something. "I don't know why I'm telling you, but I am. There's a lot of money saved up for me and Sharon – well, that's what I had in mind when I took it from the bank where I used to work. I don't think that's going to happen now."

"Like how much is a lot of money? Ten thousand quid? Twenty? Thirty thou?"

"Add a couple of noughts to the end of that last one." He watched Nick's face show surprise for the first time since they had met.

"Three million smackers? Hasn't anyone missed it?"

"It's money that doesn't really exist. I mean that no-one's going to miss it, really. See, at a bank, there's lots of dormant accounts. That's what they call the accounts that haven't been touched for fifteen years or so. Usually they're savings accounts. Sometimes the account holders just die, and the people left behind have no idea that the accounts ever even existed."

"So what's meant to happen to it? This is getting to

be fun, this is." Nick looked at Leo over the top of his mug of tea.

"Look, I don't want to be rude or anything, but you said you're meant to be playing tonight. Aren't you meant to be rehearsing or something?"

"Bugger that. I know the set backwards. Chaz, my roadie, can play almost as well as I can for the sound-check. He's such an ugly fucking bastard, though, that there's no way he could go on stage for me. Shame, he's a good kid. Go on with your story. It's getting in-teresting." There was a quiet intensity in Nick's voice. "Before you do, though, you hungry? I am. I could murder a plate of poached egg and baked beans on toast. You?"

Leo was suddenly aware that he hadn't eaten anything at breakfast. He'd been too busy arguing with Gail. His stomach seemed to have settled down a bit. "Sounds good." Nick called the order to Ernie, and then leaned forward. "So tell me," he said.

"So what's meant to happen is that after fifteen years, the money in a dormant account gets shifted to a com-mon pool and it all goes to deserving causes." This was the first time he'd ever explained to anyone what he'd done, and it felt good.

"And you thought you were a deserving cause?"

"None better." Leo's voice took on a new strength. "You see, someone had put me in charge of this sort of thing. Managing the dormant accounts, I mean. And if you know what you're doing with the computers, it's quite easy to cook the books. You simply fake a withdrawal just before the last one, which was fifteen years ago, and transfer the money to another account, which was set up more than fifteen years ago, and then was closed just over five years ago – I mean that's what the records show when you've finished with them. And while that account was active, it transferred the money into another account, somewhere safe. But all the records have been destroyed when the account was closed. So no-one knows where the money is now."

"Pretty smart. Which bank do you work for?"

"Did work," Leo corrected him. "I got made redundant a few months back. Over six months, really. More like a year ago, actually, if I'm going to be honest with you. Austerity measures, they said. Been living on the redundancy pay since then. Bastards."

"Tough shit. Which bank was that, then?"

Leo told him.

"Holy fuck, that's where I keep my money. How many more like you are there working there, ripping off these dormant accounts?"

"Hard to say. I'd be willing to bet that there's someone like me working in all the banks, though, doing the same thing."

"I guess it adds up pretty fast."

"Takes a bit of time and patience. I never take more than a couple of thousand out of an account at any one time."

"Still, a thousand here, a couple of thousand there. Pretty soon you're talking real money."

"Right." The eggs and beans arrived, and they applied themselves to the food. Halfway through the toast, Leo looked up. "Why are you helping me, and why am I telling you all this?"

"Because I'm a nice guy, that's why. Answers both questions, doesn't it?"

"OK. What are you going to do about it?" Nick looked at him. "I mean, I've just told you about a bloody great felony that I have committed. Aren't you going to tell the police? Or someone?"

Nick raised his voice. "Hey, Ernie! My friend Leo's just nicked three million quid from a bank."

"Good for him," came the reply. "Serve the bastards right, crooked load of buggers that they are. Reckon he's going to be the one paying for the tea and toast, then?" He chuckled.

"No, I still have my pride, thank you," said Nick. "See," he said, lowering his voice, "most people couldn't give a toss."

"Police would."

"Sure they would. How long would it take them to prove anything without a confession from you?"

"Point."

"Right then, the answer is, I'm not going to tell anyone right now, except Ernie, who I've just told, and daft old sod that he is, he took it as a joke. The question is, where is this money?"

"Japan."

"Ja-fucking-pan?"

"It seemed like a good idea at the time. I wanted somewhere where if anyone started sticking their noses into things around, they wouldn't find it easy to get around, because of the language."

"And you, of course, have no problem with that?" Nick sounded sarcastic, but Leo took it in his stride.

"As a matter of fact, that's correct," Leo answered. "I speak and read Japanese pretty well. Can't write it that well, but okay. Studied it at uni along with computer science."

Nick sat back and looked at him. "You do? Well, well."

"What's that meant to mean, for God's sake?"

"Just that we have a Japanese tour starting next week,

and no-one in the crew who speaks a bloody word of the lingo. Come on, let's get out of here. I'm paying," he said, and bustled over to Ernie, where some sort of transaction took place.

"Where are we going?" Leo asked.

"County Hall, where the gig's on tonight."

"Not this way, we're not."

"We are if I say we are. Come on. Now tell me, Leo," and Nick's face turned to face him, the eyes now hidden behind a pair of mirrored aviator shades, "tell me just how you are going to get your three million nicker out of Nippon."

"Fly over there and withdraw it in cash, in US dollars. Then fly off to the Caymans and start a company there, with three million minus chump change capital. And take it from there." Nick was shaking his head. "What's wrong?"

"Mate, you are out of your tiny little mind. World-class specialist in Oriental languages, perhaps, computer genius you are, maybe, and somewhere in the final running for Thief of the Year, but you haven't got your head screwed on, have you?"

"Uh?"

"Didn't you tell me just now that your wallet was with your wife, or your ex-wife, or whatever she is to you now?"

Leo stopped short. His mouth literally dropped open.

"I thought that was just one of those meta-things till I saw you just now," said Nick. "Shut it. You look stupid."

"Metaphors. I've got no money to get over there, have I?"

"Right, sunshine. No chequebook, no credit cards, no cash. Unless your Gail has been nice about things, and kept her hands off it."

"Can you call her and find out? Say you're a friend of mine or something?"

"That wouldn't be far off the truth now, would it?"

Leo fished in his pocket and pulled out his mobile. He turned it on, and thumbed the keys. "No signal here," he said.

"What company? Oh, them. Same as me. I'm getting a signal here."

They compared phones. "Same model. And mine says No Service and yours has four bars. Bloody hell! The bitch has stopped my phone, I bet. Use yours?"

Nick handed Leo his phone, and dialled Gail's mobile number before handing it back.

Nick held the phone against his ear, a lazy smile on his face. "Yes, Gail? No, you don't know me, but I'm Nick, a friend of Leo's. Yeah, he's okay, just can't come to the phone right now. No, honest, he's okay. Look, the thing is, he said he'd left his wallet at home. Any way I can come round and collect it?" His face changed. "You did what? Why? Well, that's your privilege, I suppose." He mashed the keys and put the phone back in his pocket. "Silly bitch has shredded your cards and your chequebook. Put them down the garbage disposal, and then burned the rest of the crap she found in there, she says." He shrugged. "Women, can't live with them, can't live without them, can you?"

"So what happens now? How do I get to Japan? It's one of those accounts where you have to show up in person to do things."

"And in the meantime? Your best bet is to become one of the Killer Rabbits and help us out on the Japanese tour. That will get you where you want. You know something about guitars? Great. We can use you.

Bobby gets through top E strings like they're going out of style. If you can get a new string on and tuned in less than 20 seconds, Bobby will be your lifetime friend. Which, as I said, isn't likely to be very long, seeing as how the galloping syph is galloping pretty bloody fast right now and the antibiotics seem to have given up the fight, but still, gratitude's what it is, isn't it?"

"Visa? Passport? Luggage, spare clothes?"

"We can take care of that sort of thing. We're not the biggest band in the world, but I tell you, those Japanese are paying a lot of money for the privilege of seeing us thrash out a few simple bar chords and hear Leo – that's our Leo, not you – hit the drums. I think we'll be able to squeeze you into the tour without too much trouble."

"Well, thanks."

"Been to Japan before, then, have you?"

"Three times. Tokyo, Osaka, Kyoto, Nagoya, Sapporo, Nagasaki."

"Great. No problem getting you on the tour. You're our location tour manager or something, then. Fix us up with the booze and the women or whatever we need to keep us happy. Change Bobby's E strings as well, and everyone's happy, right?"

"No drugs in Japan, you know that?"

"Oh come off it, of course there are drugs there, aren't there? Bit of dope, whatever?"

"Yes, but you don't want to do them. Unless you fancy a Japanese prison for a few years while they decide what to do with you. Believe me, you don't want that. They're crazy about that sort of thing, especially when it comes to famous foreigners. Look at what happened to Paul McCartney."

"Better tell all the lads, then. Don't want to spend hours in police stations getting them out."

"Days, or years, more like," said Leo.

"Nah, I'm joking," said Nick. "Our lot doesn't do drugs. If they do, they're out. Pig sees to that."

A rock band that doesn't do drugs? What were they? Some sort of weird Christian sect? And who or what was Pig?

They walked on together for a while, and then Leo turned to Nick. "What do you want out of this?"

"Like I said, I'm a nice guy. I'm not going to insist on anything. I'll just gently remind you that one man doesn't need that much money, especially if he has no-one else to spend it on."

"You're a hell of a guy, Nick," Leo said after a hundred yards' more walking.

"Ain't I just? You should see my halo when I've just polished it. Nah, I'm just an ordinary schmuck whose fingers bend into the right shapes, and who was lucky enough to meet the right people at the right time." They turned the corner. "See, there's the County Hall," said Nick. "Told you we were going there. Just took the scenic route, that's all. Let's get in there and turn you into a Killer Rabbit."

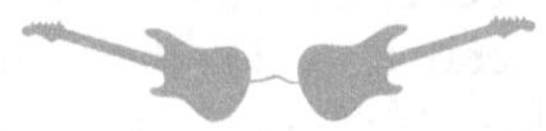

Chapter 3

All the action was backstage, in a maze of corridors and dressing rooms. Leo soon lost his bearings, but Nick seemed to know what he was doing. They came to a room where there were about twenty people, it seemed to Leo, all wearing the official Killer Rabbits tour T-shirt, and most wearing the same sort of greasy jeans that Nick was wearing. Some looked Indian, some were black, and there was one Chinese, by the look of him. There were a couple of women in the group.

"Here, you miserable load of bastards," Nick yelled at them. "Meet Leo. He's going to take us round Japan. And he's just stolen three million pounds from a bank, so he's a good guy." There was a faint ironic cheer from the mob (as Leo saw them).

"Are you fucking mad?" he said to Nick as loudly as he dared. "Telling the world I've stolen three million pounds."

"It's the best way of keeping them off your back."

"How do you mean?"

"No-one's ever going to believe that you actually stole

three million quid. It's a joke, right? Then if the police or anyone come looking, everyone's just going to say, 'Oh yeah? Leo the bank robber? Ha bloody ha.' Get it?"

"Sort of."

"Except your name isn't going to be Leo in a while."

"Oh?"

"Once you're one of the Rabbits, you get a new name. Everyone does. Except for us, the band, that is."

"What's mine going to be, then?"

"Not my decision. That's up to Pig there." Nick jerked his thumb towards a massive biker type who looked as though he wrestled grizzly bears for a hobby, or perhaps as practice for mugging little old ladies and robbing them of their old age pensions. "This is Pig. I mentioned him to you back then. Pig's our people person. Or if you want to be posh about it, he's our HR manager."

Leo regarded the man-mountain with suspicion. "Him?"

"Been with us more than ten years now. Great guy. I'll take you over and introduce you."

Leo had always considered himself to be a tall man, but Pig managed to intimidate him with his sheer size and bulk. He had at least three inches' advantage over Leo in terms of height, and his chest was probably twice as far round. His Killer Rabbits T-shirt had to be custom-made, Leo thought. They didn't make them that size in the factory, did they?

Pig looked down at him. It was an unfamiliar sensation. "Leo the Bank Robber?"

"It wasn't a piggy bank," Leo said, taking a chance that this beast would have a sense of humour.

It only seemed to take Pig a second to catch on, but

Leo's worst fears went unrealised. "Better not catch you stealing from my bank, mind you," Pig warned Leo, extending a large paw. "Shake."

Leo's hands weren't small, but his right hand felt like a child's as the mass of meat and muscle at the end of Pig's arm enveloped it. There was a pressure that felt as though it could convert his hand to hamburger if Pig chose, but it eased off at the critical moment. Pig released his grip, and Leo rubbed his right hand as unobtrusively as he could manage.

"Crane," Pig said, after a few seconds of looking Leo up and down. "That's what you are. Crane."

"Bird or machine?" asked Nick, who'd been watching with some amusement.

"Eh? Oh, both. Skinny tall things, the both of them. So, Crane, you're going to take us to Japan?" Leo nodded. "Speak the language, do we? Alligayto and all that?"

"*Hai*," said Leo and bowed in the best Japanese fashion he could manage.

"Good start, anyway. What do you know about this stuff?" Pig jerked his thumb towards the mass of sound equipment and instruments.

Nick replied. "He knew about Betty here," tapping the guitar case. "Guessed she was a 335 rather than a 330, but not bad, considering the case was closed and he couldn't see her. I'm off now. See you later, Crane, Pig."

Pig nodded approvingly. "Sounds as though you're going to fit in as soon as we get you dressed right. Where's your clobber?"

"That's a bit tricky to explain."

Pig put his head on one side. "So explain. I'm waiting."

"Well, you see, I've sort of left my wife and my

girlfriend – well, I thought she was my girlfriend, but it seems she isn't really…"

"And the wife has changed the locks, so you can't get into your house? And the stuff you had at the girlfriend's? She won't let you in."

"Yeah, you're right about the girlfriend. The wife hasn't had time to change the locks, I think. I only walked out on her this morning." Pig raised his shaggy eyebrows. "Well, I suppose I didn't know I was walking out when I left the house. But it seems that my mind's been made up for me. She's trashed my cards and my chequebook. Nick called the house for me."

Pig's head moved slowly from side to side. "Nick. Lovely bloke. Always helping lame ducks over stiles."

"Don't you mean lame dogs?"

"I know what I mean. I know a lame duck when I see one, Crane. So I suppose you want one of us to go and talk to your old lady and get your stuff for you?"

"Well, I'll need my passport and a couple of other things. It's not just a toothbrush and a spare pair of socks."

Pig laughed. "Passport? Scuzz will fit you up with a new passport as soon as he gets here. Some time this afternoon, he said. What's the other shit?"

"A Japanese seal. Sort of stamp with my name carved in the end. Banks and things in Japan use them instead of signatures."

"And you have a bank account over there where you need that sort of thing?"

Leo nodded. "And whatever passport this Scuzz is going to give me won't work with the bank. I'm going to have to prove myself to them. And that means my real passport."

"No driving licence or anything like that?"

"All in my wallet, which she's probably burned by now. No, it's got to be the passport."

Pig sighed. "OK, I'll get a couple of the lads to go down and get the stuff. Tell me where the house is, what shit you need, and where you keep it."

"Shall I write it down?"

"Nah. I'll remember. Try me."

Leo spent about five minutes telling Pig what he thought he might need, and as best as he could remember, where it was in the house.

"Okay," said Pig when Leo ran out of breath, "just check that this is what you want," and proceeded to give a completely accurate replay of what he had just been told.

"Pretty smart there," said Leo.

"You were going to say 'for a greasy biker', weren't you?" said Pig, and grinned. "Actually, I'm pretty dumb for a PhD."

"You have a PhD?" asked Leo, incredulously.

"Sure. Fluid mechanics. Boring as shit. This is a lot more fun. Pays better, too. Nick and the lads are good people, let no-one tell you any different. Keep it quiet, though, will you? I like being the big dumb bastard most of the time."

"No problem," said Leo. This was going to be interesting, he thought. A lot more interesting than the bank.

"Thanks. Hey, what do you want to eat? All your food is on the Rabbits, by the way. And a place to sleep, but a lot of the time it's in the Rabbit Hutch." Whatever that meant, Leo thought. "And you'll get paid. Nick talk to you about money?"

"No."

"Never does. Expects me to sort these things out for

him, bless his little heart. Okay, we'll leave it as a surprise for you. A nice one, that is, if you do your job right, and you're as good as Nick seems to think you are.

"Thanks."

"Thank Nick when you see him next. Hey, Chick!" he called to a man who was passing. He appeared to be Indian. "What's cooking? Chick here does all the cooking for us. Hope you like Indian, because that's all we eat."

"Shrimp korma or beef vindaloo," the Indian told him.

"You're asking me which I want?"

"I know what you're wanting. You're going to be having the vindaloo. But what about...?"

"This is Crane," said Pig.

"And I'll have the korma," said Leo.

"Wimp." Pig grinned through his beard.

"Why Chick?" Leo asked, when Chick had left them.

"Short for Chicken," said Pig. "All right," as Leo looked baffled. "Chicken's short for Chicken Tikka Masala, but that's a bit long, so he's Chick now. Okay? Bet your name doesn't stay at being Crane, either. But right now, that's who you are. Now it's time for you to get your shirt, and meet the rest of the Rabbits."

"Before that, where do I go for a piss in this place?"

Pig jerked his thumb at a door. Leo found a smelly row of urinals, one stall, and a washbasin at which Sharon, stripped to the waist, was washing her face. He recognised the long blonde hair and the well-remembered shape of her back.

"What the hell are you doing here, Sharon?" he asked before he could stop himself.

The bearded, long-haired blond man at the washbasin

turned round and looked at Leo. "Sharon? Who the fuck is Sharon?"

"Oh shit. Sorry," Leo mumbled. "You just reminded me of…"

"Forget it." The other put out a wet hand to shake. "Just joined us? Good to see you. I'm Duck. As in 'couldn't give a flying'."

"And I'm Crane."

"Good to meet you. You're going to be taking this gang of infants around Japan, is that what I heard?"

"Looks like it. Wasn't what I had planned when I got up this morning, though."

"Life's full of that sort of thing. Didn't Kierkegaard have something to say about that? Something like 'Life is not a problem to be solved, but a reality to be experienced'?"

"Who?" For the second time that day, Leo discovered his jaw had literally dropped with surprise.

"Soren Kierkegaard. Danish philosopher. Nineteenth century. Don't tell me you've never heard of him, you ignorant peasant."

"Yes, of course I've heard of him, but I've never read any of his writing."

"You should. It will sort things out for you."

"And I only came here for a piss," Leo grumbled to himself as he unzipped and let the warm stream flood down the drain. "Not to be told about bloody Scandinavian philosophers."

"So you met Duck?" said Pig when Leo came out. "He told me you never read any Kierkegaard. That right?"

Leo nodded, obscurely ashamed of being backstage with the road crew of a world-famous rock band, and not having read any of a nineteenth-century Danish philosopher's writings.

"Well, that's not a problem," said Pig. "Neither have I. Duck's always showing off his master's in philosophy."

"Do you all have letters after your names?"

Pig considered for a moment. "No, there's one or two haven't."

"Chick?"

"Chick's a bloody wizard with computers, man. Graduated top of his class, and then said he was bored with computers and wanted a real challenge. Got into cooking and listening to the Rabbits. Came along back-stage one evening after a gig with this bloody great pot of dopiaza and another of butter masala, and piles of naan, which he dished out to everyone and then asked if there was a job for him with the Rabbits. Course, Nick said "yes", soft-hearted git that he is. Always picking up trash from the streets and helping them. No offence meant there, mind," he added quickly as Leo bristled. "Chick's done wonders for the light show as well. Got it all running off one little laptop now, when we used to have to take around three bloody great boxes be-fore. Duck there, he's a genius when it comes to doing the monitor mix that the band hear on stage. Wouldn't believe that went with existentialism, would you? And Scuzz, who you're going to meet, well, he's got this de-gree in something weird, like paleogeology, but he's a wizard when it comes to official papers. You'll see."

"I get your point," Leo said. "Killer Rabbits is just one giant collection of untapped talent."

"Right. You got it. And it's not always the one you ex-pect. Now take you, for example. You speak Japanese, you probably understand computers and money, and you spotted Nick's guitar in its case. There's something there for sure, and the Rabbits will probably find out what it is."

"You're making Killer Rabbits sound like a religious group or something."

Pig stroked his beard. "Well, I suppose we are a group. We tend to stick together even when there isn't a tour on. Not saying we're one big happy family all the time, though. We have our share of disagreements. But this isn't getting you dressed properly. Here, catch," and he threw a bundle to Leo.

The bundle was composed of two Killer Rabbits crew T-shirts rolled together. "Should be your size," said Pig. "You're meant to wear one all the time over whatever else you want to wear when you're with us. You can have as many of these as you need, but only two a week. Throw them out when they're dirty – we don't bother washing them. You'll find out about all the rest of life with us in a bit. Come on, get one of those on you, and let's eat."

What the hell had he got himself into? Leo asked himself as he rolled the T-shirt over his head. Was this some sort of mad genius cult or what was it? He followed Pig down the corridor to one of the innumerable backstage rooms, where the Rabbits sat on folding chairs round a couple of large steaming pots of curry, balancing disposable dishes on their laps and digging in with plastic spoons, and chasing the sauce with wedges of Indian bread.

The korma was good – very good. Clad in his new Killer Rabbits T-shirt, Leo felt there could be worse ways to live. No-one spoke to him, or even seemed to notice his existence, but that seemed to be normal. These people were concentrating on eating, and conversation would have been a distraction, it seemed.

He looked around for Nick, or the other members of the band, whom he felt sure he would recognise, but the only people in the room seemed to be crew.

"Come on," said Pig, when he'd finished two bowls of korma, and Pig had managed to sink four of vindaloo. "Time to meet Scuzz."

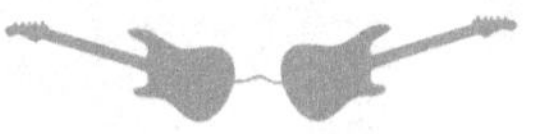

Chapter 4

Scuzz turned out to be only a little older than Leo, but he appeared to be middle-aged, going on elderly. He seemed to be formally dressed in a three-piece suit, complete with watch-chain, but the waistcoat was a skilfully converted Killer Rabbits crew T-shirt, and when he stood up to shake hands, he turned out to be wearing denim Bermuda shorts. As he released Leo's hand, his pink bow tie lit up and spun round three times.

"We make an exception for Scuzz here," Pig explained to Leo, who was staring at Scuzz's outfit, and was still somewhat in shock at the behaviour of the tie.

"Crane here needs a new passport," Pig told Scuzz. "We're off to Japan next week."

"Correction," said Scuzz. He had a strangely dry, dusty sort of voice. "You are off to Japan. I'm staying here."

"We'll talk about that later," said Pig. "I'm going to leave Crane with you, and you can sort things out. Before four o'clock, though. I'm going to want him after that."

"So what sort of passport do you want?" Scuzz asked Leo when they were alone.

"What do you mean, what sort? The usual kind. Anyway, I've got a passport already. Pig's going to arrange for it to be brought from my house – my wife's house."

"I meant, what nationality?"

"I have a choice? Why can't I go under my own name?"

"Tradition," replied Scuzz. "Except for the band, no-one uses their own names to travel. Now what's it going to be?" He opened a box and started flipping through its contents. "Better be an EU passport, don't you think? No problems getting into Japan with any of those. You've never had a fancy to be Albanian, I take it? No? Didn't think you had. Turkish? No, I don't think you'd pass as Turkish, somehow. Now Belgian, that's a fine thing to be," holding up a red passport.

"Where do all these come from?" asked Leo, as he looked at the box full of passports of different colours.

"Festivals, mostly. Amazing what people drop on the ground or leave behind in their tents when they're watching the bands. We got fifty-six out of last Glastonbury alone. Here you are, Crane, you can be Gilles Fontaine, aged 32. Seems a good match. And it's not a biometric passport, either, so we're all right there, aren't we? He even looks a bit like you." He flipped the passport over to Leo, who examined it. The face that looked out could be taken as a bad caricature of his own, he supposed.

"If this is lost," he said to Scuzz after a few minutes' thought, "then the number's going to be on their shit-lists, isn't it?" Scuzz nodded. "And so the first time I go through a border where they actually check the bloody thing, I'm going to be whisked off and put in the slammer while they decide how many years I should get for impersonating a Belgian."

"That all sounds perfectly reasonable," said Scuzz. He paused. "That is, of course, if the number on the passport you present is the same as the one on the passport which was lost and reported stolen." He waited for the penny to drop.

"I take it you've done this before?" said Leo.

Scuzz laughed. "You mean today? No, actually, you're the first one today, but the," he counted on his fingers, "seventh one so far this week. And I can assure you that no-one has ever been stopped for questioning with one of my passports."

"But you're not travelling," Leo objected. "You said to Pig you weren't coming to Japan with us." He realised he'd said "us", meaning the Rabbits, without thinking about it. It must be the effect of the T-shirt, he reasoned.

"I always say I'm not coming. Hate flying, that's why. Pig always makes me come along anyway. Last time it took quarter of a bottle of whisky and three barbiturates, and they carried me on as hand luggage."

"Don't believe you," said Leo, defiantly.

"Well, slight exaggeration, perhaps, but I was definitely on a higher plane of existence than the rest of humanity while I got onto the plane, and all the way to New York. Now, business. You'll want a driving license, of course. Monsieur Fontaine forgot to lose his at the same time he lost his passport, careless bugger, so we'll have to do a bit of work there. No worries. Want to drive a 3-ton or 10-ton or one of the really big bastards?"

"What?"

"What size lorry, or truck as our transatlantic friends call those big smelly things, do you want to be licensed for?"

Leo, who had never driven anything bigger than a Ford Focus, told Scuzz firmly that he was content with just an ordinary car license.

"At least let me give you a fork-lift truck certificate," pleaded Scuzz. "That could be really useful at times, you know." With some misgivings, Leo allowed himself to be persuaded. "I'll get you all the other stuff as well," Scuzz told him. "National ID card, no problem, as the Japanese aren't going to have the chip reader installed. Health insurance cards. No problem. Fine, just look this way a moment, would you?"

Leo obliged, and Scuzz produced a small camera, and took one or two photos. "Fine, and we're finished before four. Pig's going to be pleased. So bugger off, and find him. Not sure what he wants you for, but if he says he wants you, you'd better listen."

Feeling completely bewildered, Leo made his way out of the room into the corridor. This wasn't happening to him, he told himself. He was the one who made the decisions, as Gail had reminded him only that morning. Was it really only that morning? A lot seemed to have happened already that day. And now he wasn't making any decisions at all. He seemed to have been kidnapped by a gang of lunatics, who cheerfully went around breaking whatever conventions and laws they felt like. Could he just take off the Killer Rabbits T-shirt, and make his way out of the building and never see them again?

Somehow he doubted whether that was the case, even if he had somewhere to go to. A return to Gail was out of the question, almost certainly. Sharon was also a no-go area. And he had no money and no visible means of support. Did he even want to leave this bunch of nut-cases, anyway? They seemed friendly enough, at least. Might as well go with the flow, and see what washed up. At least it looked as though he would get to Japan with them.

While he was thinking along these lines, he was startled out of his reverie by Pig's giant hand descending on his shoulder. "Time to meet Bobby," said Pig.

Bobby was the Killer Rabbits' second guitarist. He didn't have the star quality that Nick had, though some critics claimed his licks were more musical, if less technical. Typically, he stood at the back of the stage, as if avoiding the light, with his face almost turned away from the audience. His spare frame was often silhouetted against the stage backdrop, but it was rare to see any details. When it came to band photos, there usually seemed to be something in the way, obscuring his face, often his longish hair, and he was hardly ever seen off-stage. The music press had put forward all kinds of lurid theories to explain his reclusive nature, but Leo had never believed any of them. Mind you, Nick had warned him of Bobby's syphilis. Didn't that eat away at your nose, or something disgusting? That would explain why he was never photographed or spotlit on stage.

"I'll let Nick introduce you," said Pig, as they swung round a corner. "Bobby's shy around me," he added. "Shy around almost everyone, come to that," he said, confirming some of Leo's suspicions. "Here you go," he said to Nick, who popped out of a dressing-room door to meet them. "He's all yours."

"If he plays his cards right, he's all Bobby's," said Nick. "OK, let's go," he said to Leo. "Try not to be surprised by anything. It will upset Bobby if you look surprised."

He knocked on another door, and a soft voice told them to come in.

"Bobby, dear," said Nick. "I've brought you Crane, who's just joined us. He tells me that he can change guitar strings."

Bobby's back was to them, sitting in front of a dressing-room mirror, head slumped, face hidden by a mane of dark, almost black, hair. As Leo watched, Bobby's neck slowly straightened, and he got his first look at Bobby's face in the mirror. It wasn't what he expected. It was a soft, delicate face, quite attractive, he supposed, if you went for that sort of thing.

"Thanks, Nick darling," said Bobby without turning round. "He's a bit tall, isn't he?"

"Well, so are you, dear," replied Nick. "But that's what you like, isn't it?"

What was all this dearing and darlinging, Leo wondered. Nick didn't seem gay. Was he just humouring Bobby with all this camp stuff? Had he been brought here to serve as the boy toy for some rich rock star queen, or what? Like most men of his generation, Leo considered himself to be fairly broad-minded. He had some gay friends, supported their right to marry, had even (though he didn't tell anyone about this) gone to bed with a couple of male friends when he was at university, but now considered himself to be as heterosexual as any. Probably Bobby was a nice person, he thought, but if he starts making moves towards me, I'm just going to have to turn him down. Nicely, politely, but the answer's going to have to be "no". And that's the end of my time with the Rabbits, I guess. Shame. Just when I was getting used to the idea and I could see my way to collecting the money from Japan.

"All right, leave us together," said Bobby in that soft husky voice. Leo started rehearsing the words of refusal and working out his escape route to the door. "Let's see you change a string. I break a lot of them, you know. Did Nick tell you? I only like .008s, and they can only take so much bending. The guitar's over there. It's my second-best Telecaster, so be careful with it, won't you? There's a box of strings by it." The voice was almost seductive, Leo said to himself. But he wasn't going to let himself be talked into anything.

Well, this is delaying the evil hour, Leo thought, as he went over to pick up the guitar, and a string in an envelope. Changing guitar strings was actually something he did quickly and quite well. Some time ago, a friend had taught him "the Martin knot", which, if you do it properly, is the fastest and most efficient way to do it. Through the peg, round and under, loop up and round, and turn. It took him less than thirty seconds, he reckoned, as he admired his handiwork.

"Twenty-seven seconds," came that slow husky voice. "Very good indeed." The voice seemed louder than before. Leo looked up from the guitar. Bobby had got up from the chair and was standing close behind him. "Looks good, too," Bobby added, bending forward and inspecting the instrument. The smell of Bobby's hair filled Leo's nostrils. It was a clean smell, which seemed out of place compared to the rather greasy, grimy atmosphere of the other Rabbits. He had a good view of Bobby's left ear, pierced for a small diamond stud. "Very nice," said Bobby. "Very good. Good boys get a kiss."

Oh no, he was going to have to fight this one off. "I'm not really into this sort of thing," he stammered. "I think there's been a mistake. I'd better go." He turned towards the door.

There was a sigh from behind him as he reached for the door handle. "Oh, you're not one of those ones who prefers men, are you? Nick never gets these things wrong, so I don't see how you could be."

"Sorry. What are you saying?"

"I am asking you if you're gay, you stupid man."

"No, but…"

"Then you won't object, will you? Turn round and look at me, for God's sake." There was a snap in Bobby's voice, and Leo turned to obey.

"Oh," was all he could manage. It was obvious now that Bobby was a woman. A tall, somewhat masculine woman, with a distinct lack of curves in some places, but still clearly a woman, now that her hair was back and he could see her face clearly. Actually, rather a nice face, he said to himself. One he certainly didn't mind kissing or being kissed by. He accepted the peck on the cheek, actually feeling rather cheated that it wasn't more intimate. He noticed her eyes; dark brown, with long lashes and no obvious make-up, which gave them a sort of naked look.

"That's enough for now," said Bobby.

As soon as she had kissed him, though, Leo remembered what Nick had told him about Bobby's disease, and he unconsciously flinched. Bobby noticed the move, and smiled.

"Oh, I see," she said. "Nick's been telling you I've got some foul and horrible disease, has he? What was it this time? Ebola? Lassa fever?" She was smiling, for the first time since Leo had met her. A rather pleasant and attractive smile.

"Syphilis," Leo mumbled.

"The bastard," she said, but still smiling.

"Why on earth would he...?" and Leo fought back a number of answers which came to his mind, but simply asked, "Why do you keep... how do I say it...? a secret?"

"Oh, Nick's got a weird sense of humour for a start, and to protect me, to answer your other question."

"Why you keep it secret that you're a woman, you mean?"

"Exactly. This is a man's world, this music biz, for the most part. The women in it are so often just decorative objects, and have to flash their tits or something to make it, even when they're the smart ones, like Lady Gaga, or talented, like Neko Case or someone."

"You think Lady Gaga's smart? Can't stand her music."

"Nor me," Bobby said, "but she's one smart cookie, in the way David Bowie or Salvador Dali was smart. New name, new image every year, touch of enigma, a lot of bi sex, and some real talent to go with it all, though it's not something I go for myself. Me, I really love the kind of thing that the Rabbits are playing, this sort of post-punk blues/soul fusion stuff. I've always loved it, since I was a little skinny kid with braces, and when big brother Nick started playing guitar, I begged our parents to buy me one too, and he and I used to jam along together. Me on this cheap crappy Woolworth's thing, and him on a slightly better Jap-crap Les Paul copy."

"Nick's your brother? He doesn't look like you."

"Half-brother. Different fathers, so different genes and different names. His dad ran off and Mum remarried."

"And then?"

"Nick's really bloody good at what he does. He never

wanted to do anything other than play in a band. And little sister Roberta – that's where the Bobby comes from – wanted to do the same. I'm almost as good as he is."

"Some say you're better."

"Whatever." She shrugged. "Anyway, I'm this great gawk of a thing. I mean, look at me." She spread her hands and ran them down her body. "A figure like a stick, and that's a big long stick, a face that looks like Keith Richards in drag or something—"

"Hey," Leo interrupted. "I like your face."

"Sweet of you to say so, darling, but it's not going to launch a thousand ships, or sell a thousand albums, is it now, with the best will in the world? Anyway, there was that, and there was the fact that I am a pretty shy person – well, not shy so much as I'm allergic to people in large quantities. So the idea of becoming a rock star really wasn't me. But what else could I do that I was good at? So when Nick and his mates started the band that turned into the Rabbits, little sis came along and started playing along, and the lads loved it. One of them tried to love me as well, but I wasn't having any of that."

Leo wondered exactly what she meant by that last. Was she a lesbian, or did she just mean that she didn't like that particular man?

"Anyway," she continued, "I played on their first two studio albums, though you won't find my name anywhere, but when they went on the road with those songs, everyone said there was something missing from the sound – me."

"So Nick persuaded you to join the band?"

"Basically, under my own set of very weird conditions. I'm a very screwed-up person, you know."

"That's all right. So am I," Leo found himself saying. Actually, he'd always thought of himself as being the normal one. It was other people who were screwed up, in his opinion, but he wanted to know more about Bobby, and this seemed to be the right sort of thing to say to get her to talk more. Actually, now he looked at her a bit closer, she seemed quite interesting, in a bedroom sort of way. Some sharp angles there, but that's what he always liked, if Sharon, and Gail when they first met, come to that, were any guide.

She shot him a glance. "Yeah, that's what Nick said to me. Or did he say you'd screwed up?" There was more than a hint of mockery in the smile she now gave in his direction. "Anyway, so here I am, second guitarist with the Killer Rabbits, man of mystery. Except I'm not a man. Hardly seen on stage, never off-stage, face always hidden. Never give face-to-face interviews, always email or texts. Some of the Rabbits maybe don't know who I really am, even. So here I am. Pretty fucked up, wouldn't you say?"

This was really pretty weird, Leo told himself. "So why tell me?"

"Nick told me that you were pretty fucked up yourself. I think he sees you as some sort of pet for me to take care of. Take me out of myself or some sort of crap like that. And you seem to know your way round guitars. That's your job for tonight, to look after my guitars. Change strings, make sure the pedals are all set up right, that sort of thing. It's all written down somewhere, so don't worry because you don't know what you're doing the first night. Anyway, Chaz, Nick's roadie, will see you through the first few times." She paused. "Also, you're taller than me."

"Does that matter?"

"I can't fancy men who are shorter than me."

Jesus, this was all moving too fast for him. "Do you fancy me, then?"

She sent another strangely shy smile his way. "Not yet. But if you turn out to be nice, who knows what might happen?"

This is totally crazy, Leo told himself. From being an unhappily married man with a bit on the side, I've gone to being the pet and potential boy toy of a rock star with a gender identity crisis. "Unreal," he said aloud.

"It's real," she grinned. "And you're not going to walk out, because you need to get to Japan."

"Nick told you? I suppose so, since he seems to be telling everybody."

"Yeah, but he's telling everyone as a sort of joke. He does that sort of thing a lot. Tells the craziest stories, and everyone thinks he's bullshitting them, until they turn out to be true. You're not bullshitting him, are you? Just for a free ride to Japan or something? Because if you are, Pig and his lads will get to work on you. And whatever's left of you will regret the day you ever tried to tell a lie to the Rabbits."

"Honest, I told him about Japan before I even knew about the Japanese tour."

"It's been announced, you know. We don't exactly live under rocks. You could have found out from the papers."

"I could, but I didn't."

"OK, I believe you. Now go and ask for Chaz, and get him to show you my setup. Nick said you play yourself."

"I can make a noise. Twelve-bar in E sort of thing."

"Whatever. Feel free to play the guitars, if you want. Before the punters come in, that is. Make sure all the effects and the amps are working. And when you've done that, come back here. At least an hour before we go on stage. That means 8:30 here at the latest. Don't bother bringing me anything to eat. I throw up if I eat before a gig. Now bugger off and find Chaz. And I'd be obliged if you keep quiet about me and my little secret, if you know what I mean. Otherwise, it's the Pig and his lads treatment for you."

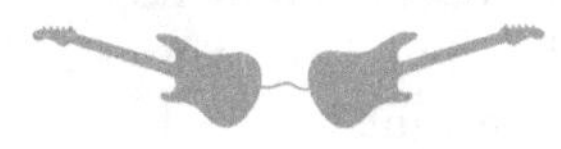

Chapter 5

Leo mumbled something and asked for Chaz, who turned out, as Nick had hinted, to be a skinny young man of surprising ugliness, who nonetheless unleashed a dazzling smile of perfect white teeth when Leo introduced himself.

"Glad you turned up," he said. "Wasn't sure if I was going to have to do both Nick's and Bobby's tonight, and it's a bugger with Bobby. He's always breaking the top strings."

'He'? Leo thought to himself. Was this some kind of a test? He wasn't going to let on either way. "So show me," he said.

They made their way onto the stage, with only a few working lights to see by. The empty County Hall auditorium, with reputedly the best acoustics in the region, stretched ahead of them into the darkness, and the PA stacks flanking both sides of the stage towered above them.

"Here you go," said Chaz, pointing to a couple of

flight cases with "Killer Rabbits – Bobby's shit" stencilled on them. "The amp's working - we did that in the sound-check, but you've got to hook up all the pedals in the pedalboard, check if anything has come loose, and then test them out. There's a cheap crap guitar in that case there for you to do it with, and there's a spare of everything if something's crapped out. There's a diagram somewhere in there to tell you where everything should go if you're not sure. And make sure you don't knock the mic in front of the speaker cabinet – it's in the right place now, and Mac will have a fit if you touch it. Check out the wireless, as well, and make sure the signal's still coming through loud and clear. You might have to change channels, as the fire service and police can break through sometimes."

"Right," said Leo, trying to absorb all this.

"And when that's done, make sure all the guitars are in tune, and arranged in the stands the way that is written there. And make sure there's enough picks. Jim Dunlop mediums, nothing fancy."

"OK," Leo said. He set to work. He'd played in bands at university, and he'd even kept a guitar and some effects pedals from that time, but Bobby's setup was an order of complexity above what he had ever encountered in the past.

Still, the neatly printed diagrams and instructions, which included the order and method for testing the effects, helped him a lot, and he found the so-called "cheap crap" guitar (which actually happened to be the same model that he had at home, wherever that was now) and plugged it in. He had a wonderful ten minutes going through the different effect settings that Bobby used, remembering some of them from the album tracks.

"Sounds good," Chaz said from the other side of the stage, when he paused. "Not your playing, I mean. That's crap. But the sound's right. Well done."

Leo turned to the guitars. There were eight of them, all told, in four pairs of identical instruments. "A spare of each, is that the idea?" he called over to Chaz.

"You got it. Bobby breaks a string, whips off the guitar, throws it at you, you pass the replacement and re-patch it into the wireless. Then you change the broken string and wait for the next time."

"How often does this happen?"

"Shouldn't be more than ten times a gig, in total. Sometimes only half a dozen times, record is twenty-three, if I remember right."

Shit! This was going to be hard work. "Can we practice just the changeover? Can you be Bobby so I can take the guitar off you and give you the new one?"

"Sure, good idea." It took a few tries, but eventually, Leo was comfortable with what he was doing, and Chaz was happy. "You're doing great for a first time."

"You been with the Rabbits long?" Leo asked him.

"Yeah, I suppose. Five, no, six years now, I suppose. It's not everyone's idea of a good time, I suppose, but it suits me."

"How so?"

"Well, we're a very tight bunch, as you've probably noticed, and Pig can be a bit of a little Hitler at times, but he's got a good side to him as well. Nick and Bobby and the boys – they're fine. Leo, the drummer – well, he's a drummer, and you can't expect anything else – but the rest of them are sweet guys to work for."

"What do you do when the Rabbits aren't touring? Work with other bands?"

"Hell, no. Once you're a Rabbit, that's what you are,

and nothing else. We get paid, even when the band's not touring, and we tend to stick together. There's the other side, you see."

"The other side?"

"Oh, sorry I spoke. Pig hasn't told you about that, then?"

"No." What the hell was all this about?

"He will, don't worry, when the time comes. Probably not too long now. Get those guitars tuned. Everything standard, except the Teles, which are in open E. EBEG#BE – got it?"

"Got it."

"You'll need to do them again just before the set, of course. Punters come in, temperature goes up, bloody things go out of tune. Keep all the spares tuned before Bobby needs them. Now let's go and get something to eat."

"Chick again?"

"Yeah." He checked his watch.

As they left the stage, one of the lights fell from the lighting truss above them. It passed so close to Leo on the way down that he could feel the wind as it fell, before smashing on the stage with a loud crash, spraying fragments of glass over Leo and Chaz, and causing them to jump out of their skins.

"Sorry," came a voice from above. "Just slipped."

"What the fuck do you think you're playing at, Lurch?" Chaz called up. "What happened to the safety?"

"It broke. Never happened before. You two okay?"

"Shaken up," said Chaz. "Watch it, won't you? And make sure every last bit of glass is swept up before the gig. Nick'll do his nut if he sees this shit lying about the place."

"Got it. Will do."

"Does this sort of thing happen often?" Leo asked Chaz. He was still shaking from the near miss.

"Never seen it happen before. We were lucky just then. Jeez." Chaz shook his head. "Come on, we haven't got a lot of time. We'll go and eat."

"We're in a hurry?"

"You've got an hour before you've got to go and see Bobby. Let's move it."

"There's a routine to this, then?"

"Yeah. Bobby gets through roadies. You're the," Chaz stopped to think, "sixth in eighteen months or so, and yes, there's a routine here."

"What happens to them if they don't make the grade?"

"Let's see, now. One went off to Australia, one now runs an undertaker's in the Isle of Man, and one seems to have just disappeared. Pig checked."

"That's three."

"Yes, well." Chaz paused. "The other two snuffed it. Topped themselves."

"Ah." There wasn't really a witty answer you could make to that.

"Don't worry," Chaz said cheerfully. "You don't look like the type who'd do that. More the undertaker in the Isle of Man type, I'd say."

"Nice to hear."

"Cheer up, it may never happen. Come on, let's join the others."

The meal was much the same as lunch, except that the chicken was tandoori chicken, and there was a chickpea masala to go with it. Again, the crew sat around in near silence, emptying their dishes. There was an almost palpable tension, and although Leo was now bursting with questions, he found it impossible to break the silence.

He was just getting up to go, when there was a loud explosive fart from the opposite side of the room.

"Now I have your attention," grinned Pig, as everyone looked up, "let's all think about tonight. You may not think it's special, because we're off to fair Nippon next week, with Crane here," and Leo found himself blushing as everyone turned to look at him, "as our fearless leader. Well, it is special. It does matter. The punters here tonight have all paid good money to see the show, and Nick and Bobby and Leo and Kevin are going to play their fucking brains out. And all of us are going to back them up to the fucking hilt. Understand me? To the fucking hilt. I don't care whether it's your first time with the Rabbits, or you've been with us ten years. You're going to give it five hundred percent. No-one fucks up. Everyone does what they're meant to do. Perfectly. Or else. Got it?" There was silence. "Got it?" more loudly.

"Got it, Pig," came the chorus.

"Now let's hear it," he growled.

On both sides of Leo, the chant started up, and grew in volume. Leo felt he had no choice but to join in. "Kill-er Rabb-its. Kill-Er Rabbits. KILL-ER RABB-ITS." Leo could imagine Roman galley slaves straining at the oars to the beat, or Egyptian slaves hauling blocks of stone up the Pyramids.

At the height of the chant, Pig clapped his hands three times, and the noise rang through the room like gunshots. The chant had stopped before the third clap, and Pig stood up. "Now let's do it!" he yelled, and the room emptied.

As Leo was leaving, Pig grabbed his arm. "How did you get on with Bobby? You okay with the way things are?"

"Er, sure."

"And no problem with what you've got to do on stage tonight? Chaz showed you how it all works, right?"

"That's fine. No worries. Well, I'm worried I'll fuck up."

"You won't. Now, about this little matter of your passport and the other shit from your house. Second set, a few of the lads who can be spared are going to go along and pay a visit. Any idea what your old lady's going to be up to around 10:30? In bed? Watching TV?"

"God knows. We usually watched TV at that time of night, but that was my choice, not hers, I guess. She might have called up one of her girlfriends and gone out to drown her sorrows at the pub."

"Or celebrate your departure?" suggested Pig. "Sorry. Any chance she'll be here tonight?"

Leo shook his head. "Doubtful. Not her sort of music."

"Well, you can't please everyone. We'll have to do the best we can, then, won't we?"

"She's not going to get hurt?"

"Not on purpose," said Pig. "If she chases us and falls downstairs, that's her lookout, isn't it? Not ours. Don't worry about it, Crane."

"All right, I believe you."

"Now go along and look after Bobby. She's a fine person." There was a slight stress on the pronoun, and Leo looked up to meet Pig's eyes, which showed a surprising compassion.

"I will, Pig. Don't worry about it." Without thinking about it, he used the same words that Pig had just used to him, and Pig replied in the same way as he had.

"I believe you," said Pig. "But if you don't…" He left the sentence dangling.

Leo made his way down the corridor to Bobby's dressing-room, and knocked on the door.

The strange soft voice, that somehow sounded sexy to him, now he knew to whom it belonged, told him to come in.

"So," Bobby said to him. She was sitting at the mirror, fooling around with makeup. She turned round, and he noticed that she was wearing a tight white T-shirt. Despite himself, he found his eyes drawn to her chest. She followed his gaze. "Not a lot there, is there?"

"So what? It's quality not quantity," he said, before realising how stupid that sounded.

"There are only two of them," she said. "How many were you expecting?"

It had been a long time since Leo had felt quite so embarrassed, and he mumbled something inconsequential to Bobby.

"Oh, never mind," she said. "I've got to get ready, and you've got to help me."

"You mean help you get dressed?"

"It would be nice if you did that. Did up a few zips and buttons here and there. But before that, I'm dying for a pee. Be a darling and make sure the coast is clear. I don't want anyone to see me with my face like this." She pointed to her half-made-up face.

Leo ducked out into the corridor, and beckoned to Bobby. "Coast clear," he said in a stage whisper. She slipped out across the corridor into the men's toilets. "Follow me, and tell me when it's safe to come back," she said.

He followed her in, and the stall door closed. He tried to close his ears to the tinkling liquid sound, which he found strangely erotic. At length there was a flushing sound, and at the same time the door opened, and one of the Rabbits walked in.

"Hi," said Leo loudly.

"Hi there. You're the new guy. Crane, isn't it?" said the other. "Excuse me if I don't shake hands," and stepped in front of the urinal. Leo stepped to the washbasin and ostentatiously ran the taps and washed his hands.

"Sorry, your name is?" Leo asked the other.

"Lurch," said the other. "I do the spots." Leo looked blank. "The spotlights. I was the silly bastard who nearly killed you just then, dropping that one on you. Sorry about that."

"Well, I'm still alive."

"Yeah, sorry," the other repeated. "Lucky. Well, gotta go," turning round and zipping himself up. "See you around, Crane."

He left, and there was a rustle from behind the stall door. "Thanks," Bobby's voice said. "Is the corridor clear?"

He looked up and down. "Yes", he said, and they slipped back into the dressing-room.

"You're not embarrassed by listening to me pee?" she said, looking him in the eye. "Or are you one of those who find it's a turn-on?" He looked away, feeling himself blushing. "Oh dear, I didn't mean to embarrass you. Don't worry, though, I'm not going to tell the world."

"What can I do for you?"

"I'll wear the leather tonight. On those hangers there. Red leather trousers, and the black and red jacket. Hot as hell under the lights, but the punters love the look, what they can see of it. And the biker boots."

Leo made his way over to the hangers and picked out the garments she had listed.

"Great. Over the back of the chair, there, please."

He turned round from placing them on the chair to see Bobby stepping out of her jeans, her long white legs almost shining under the fluorescent light. "Hand them over," she said, stretching out her hand for the trousers. He did as he was told, admiring the shape of the muscles in her thigh as they stretched up to a small, nicely shaped bottom. "That's not such a bad view, is it?" she smiled.

"It's pretty good," he smiled back. Obviously she wasn't shy about showing herself off in front of him, however shy she claimed to be in front of crowds.

"Pass me that towel," she said, pointing to a small face-towel on the dressing table. He did so, and watched as she rolled it into a cylinder and squeezed it into the crotch of her tight leather trousers. "There we are, that should put any ugly rumours to rest, shouldn't it?" She grinned at him, and pulled the T-shirt over her head, exposing a white sports bra. "Undo it for me, would you? My nails catch on the hooks."

She turned her back, and Leo fumbled with the bra strap. He noticed she had short, soft hair growing in the area around her spine, from the nape of her neck downward, which he somehow found incredibly erotic. Somehow his sweating fingers managed to undo the strap, and she slipped out of the bra, now nude from the waist up, but with her back to him. "The jacket, dear," she said, and slipped it on as Leo handed to her. "You're sweet," she said. "You didn't even try to peek. Not, as I said, that there's much to peek at, but," she turned round, having zipped up the jacket, "that bra does something, even for me. Now the shades," she added, taking a pair of aviator Ray-Bans, and slipping them on, and shaking her hair loose so that it partly covered her face. "How do I look?"

"Like Keith Richards in drag," he told her, straight-faced.

"If anyone else had quoted that back to me, I'd have slapped them silly," she said. "It's because you didn't smirk when you said it that you're forgiven. How are the guitars? All right?"

"I did everything Chaz said, and he seemed to think I'd done all right."

"Good enough for me. Well done. Now I want you to do something which you may think is a bit strange, but just bear with me. Stand facing me like that. No, a bit further away."

Leo was about to quote the title of the song by The Police to her, but sensed this was no time for joking as far as she was concerned.

"Now take my hands," she commanded him, "and close your eyes. Now feel my breathing in and out, and make your breaths coincide with mine as far as you can. Good. Nice. In. Out. In. Out."

About thirty breaths later, the little paging speaker in the corner of the room crackled. "Thirty minutes, everyone," came Pig's distorted voice.

"That means you should get backstage now," Bobby said, releasing his hands. He opened his eyes. "You're sweet," she said again. "Good luck."

"Isn't it me who's meant to be wishing you good luck?"

"Maybe, but I've done this sort of thing so many times before. This is your first time, dear." She blew him a kiss as he stepped out of the dressing-room door.

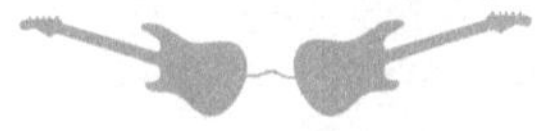

Chapter 6

The gig went well. Crouched beside Bobby's amplifier stack, a pair of earplugs stuck in his ears (courtesy of Chaz, who slipped them to him just before the band came on stage), and partly hidden a lot of the time by swirling dry ice fog, he managed to pass the right guitar at the right time, and deftly managed the string changes as needed.

Though he couldn't see Bobby's eyes behind the mirror shades, there were one or two times when she smiled at him, her back to the audience, and after the final number, before they returned for the inevitable encore, he could have sworn she blew him a kiss.

Chaz noticed the kiss, and grinned over to Leo. "OK, so you've discovered Bobby's secret already. Good for you," he shouted over the noise of the crowd, who were stamping and calling for an encore. He seemed genuinely pleased by what he had just seen.

If Chaz knew, and Pig knew, Leo asked himself, how many other people were in on the secret? Perhaps it wasn't really a secret after all, but some sort of joke designed to fool him? Whatever, Bobby attracted him, however loony the whole thing was. He knew that it wasn't up to him to make the first move, though.

The band came back and played their way through "Ladder to the Stars", the song that everyone remembered. For this number, Nick played an acoustic as he sang, and Bobby, her back to the audience, picked out sparse lead lines using the open-tuned guitar and a bottleneck slide. Though Leo knew the song as well as anyone, having bought it as a CD and a downloaded file, he felt he was hearing the song for the first time tonight, as Bobby seemed to be playing directly to him, while echoing and complementing Nick's voice and acoustic lines perfectly. Music hardly ever made him go weak at the knees, but this time, he almost had problems standing upright as the song came to an end and the band trooped off the stage, Bobby throwing her guitar to him as she went past. He only just caught it, and noticed Chaz coming over to him.

"You did great, Crane, really great. Now we have to get all this shit packed up," pointing to the guitars, pedals, cables and other musical paraphernalia on the stage. "Reckon you know where everything should go?"

"Guess so. If I don't, I'll ask you."

"Sounds good."

Leo was usually fairly well-organised, and most of the equipment seemed to fit neatly into slots cut in the foam lining the flight cases. Chaz came over and nodded. "For your first night, you've done bloody well. Get the guitars packed away. We're done for the night once you've done that, and we'll grab a beer."

It didn't take long to slot the guitars in their proper places, and lock the lid. "Pig's got the keys, don't worry," said Chaz. "Bobby's got another set. And if they both lose them, well, there's always bolt-cutters, isn't there?"

They dodged the PA crew breaking down the speaker stacks and made their way to the room where Chaz assured Leo there would be some beer. On the way, they bumped, literally, into Pig.

"We got your shit," he said to Leo. "No bones broken, you'll be pleased to hear. You'll be going to see Bobby now. Find me when you're finished, and I'll make sure you get your stuff. And all the papers that Scuzz has been doing for you."

"He was going for a beer with me," objected Chaz.

"He's going to see Bobby," Pig told them. "That's what Bobby says, anyway. And what Bobby wants, Bobby usually gets."

Leo was reminded somewhat uncomfortably of what Gail had said to him only that morning. Was it only this morning that she'd told him that they only did what he wanted? It seemed a very long time ago.

"You can take some beers with you," said Pig. "You've earned them. I was watching you. Nick picked a good'un. Well done, mate."

Leo felt as pleased with himself and as proud as he had done when he received a promotion at the bank. "Here you are," said Pig, diving into one of the rooms, and coming out with some cans of beer. "Asahi Super Dry. Got all the lads drinking this stuff. Call it acclimatisation or something."

Clutching the beer in one hand, Leo knocked on Bobby's door. He was relieved, in a way, to see that she was back in her T-shirt and jeans. She smiled as he came in. "You darling man," she said. "Come here." She extended her arms, and Leo walked towards her. "That's for being such a darling tonight," she said, throwing her arms around his neck and giving him a long kiss on the lips. "I didn't have to worry about a thing, and I can tell you that it's been a long time since then. I played 'Ladder' for you specially."

"I noticed," he said. "Thank you. It was amazing."

"Let's have a beer," she said, and reached for the pack. "Cheers," she said, and drank from the can, throwing her head back. Nice long smooth neck, Leo thought, irrelevantly. Kissable. Better not, though. He popped the top of his own can and drank.

A thought hit him. "Bobby?"

"Uh-huh?" She was leaning back in the chair with her eyes closed.

"I haven't smelled any dope or anything while I've been here. I thought it was all sex and drugs and rock and roll in this sort of situation. Where's the drugs?"

She answered him without opening her eyes. "You'd better find another band if you want something like that, darling. Nothing like that here. Rabbits need their brains unscrambled. Beer doesn't count," and she took another long swig from the can before crumpling it and throwing it with amazing accuracy into the bin, and holding out her hand for another, all without opening her eyes.

"I'm not looking for it, exactly. But I'm just surprised that there are no spliffs around here, let alone any of the other stuff."

"Well, Nick prefers wine to beer," she said, smiling. "If you are looking for a little variety, that is. But no, you're not going to find anything here. And if Pig finds you with anything like that here, you're out with a capital O. And you'll get the Pig treatment."

"Undertaker in Hull? Or worse?"

"What could be worse than being an undertaker in

Hull? Being two undertakers in Hull, I guess." She drank again. "You're okay, Crane. I don't see you ending up in Australia or anything." She put down the beer can and stretched. Leo could see she didn't shave her armpits. "Bloody hell. Rub my shoulders for me, would you? That bloody guitar strap. Go out and get some more comfortable straps for me tomorrow, will you, please." She sat up straight in her chair. "Shoulders now, please."

He stood behind her, and put his hands on her shoulders, feeling the bones beneath the thin flesh. He started rubbing and squeezing. Once upon a time, he thought, I used to do this for Gail. Once upon a time.

"A bit lower down. No, not there, here," taking his hand and putting it just below her collar-bone. "Thanks."

He continued kneading and rubbing in a reverie.

"You've got a hard-on, haven't you? I can feel it. Is it for me or her?"

He stopped rubbing immediately and looked down. His groin was nowhere near her body and her eyes were closed. And yes, he did have a hard-on. He hadn't really thought anything of it, though, until she mentioned it.

She laughed. "I didn't mean I could feel it that way. No, it was the way you are rubbing me that told me that. But there's something more, isn't there?"

"Yes." He didn't want to say any more.

"I won't say anything. I guess you should know that both Nick and I are – I guess it's not really telepathic, but more like super-empathic, if you know what I mean. We get it from our mother, who was half-Roma, and she definitely had gifts. That's why Nick's father ran away – she told him he was going to die in six months, and he thought she meant she was going to kill him."

"No?"

"No. Silly sod forgot to look where he was going, and walked under a bus in Maida Vale. Six months to the day after she'd told him, according to Mum."

Leo thought about this a little. "So how much does Nick know about me, other than what I've told him, then?"

"No idea. He just got the feeling that despite the fact that you've been a complete prick in the recent past, there's something there worth saving. A bit higher and towards my neck, please. That's better, thanks."

"It's a compliment of a sort I suppose."

"Damn right it's a compliment. Believe me, if I want to insult you, you'll know about it. That's fine, enough for now." She sat forward, and his hands dropped to his sides. "Pass me the beer." Her eyes were still closed. "And now bugger off and see Pig. I'm fine. Nick will take care of me from now on tonight. You've done a great job. Thank you." She opened her eyes and turned to smile at him. For the second time that night, he felt himself going weak at the knees. "You're a nice guy, Crane." She reached up both hands and lightly touched his temples. "You're fucked up right now, I can tell. There's a lot of pain there, but it'll go. I don't think you've made the right choices recently, but never mind. These things take time, and you're a strong man. Now leave me, please."

He was half-hoping for some sort of goodnight kiss, but it didn't seem to be on the menu, so he merely wished her a good night, and left, walking back to the room where Pig had emerged with the beer. The room was full of the Rabbits, sitting around, drinking their way through a few crates of Asahi Super Dry and talking at the tops of their voices. Leo could only catch snatches of conversation.

"…then move to the Central Committee…"

"…he's not going to like it if she gets promoted to Vice-Minister…"

"…kick the buggers between the legs, where it hurts, right in the oil fields…"

And then everything stopped.

"It's all right," Pig called out from the other corner of the room. "He's okay, Nick and Bobby say so. He'll find out enough in his own time. Crane, come over here. I've got some things for you." The conversations restarted.

Leo made his way over to Pig, who threw a can of beer in his direction. Leo noticed that Pig was drinking his beer from a glass, with a small pink plastic pig floating in it.

"That way, everyone knows not to touch my drink," said Pig. He lifted the glass, and drained it in an easy swallow, the pig bobbing against his moustache as he did so.

"Don't you ever swallow it?" Leo couldn't help asking.

"Nah. Gave up swallowing pigs a long time back." He reached in his pocket, and pulled out a British passport, and a small cylindrical case. "Your passport and your seal, sir. The rest of your shit is in the Hutch."

Leo almost grabbed them from Pig. "Thanks. I owe you."

"Oh, you do, mate, you do." Pig's laugh was a pleasant rumble. "And here is the crap from Scuzz with your Belgian passport – the one you're going to use to travel with." He passed a brown manilla envelope over to Leo. "Don't lose it, or anything in it, at least until we come back from Japan," he warned. "And don't open it here. Things will fall out. And it's all good stuff. Scuzz doesn't fuck up on these things."

Leo popped the top of his beer, and looked around. Everyone else seemed to be engrossed in their conversations. "Listen Pig, don't take this the wrong way, but who the hell are you people?"

Pig half-emptied his beer and smiled. "Well, we are a strange lot, aren't we?" He wiped the beer foam off his moustache with the back of his hand. "No dope in the corners, pretty civilised eating, this sort of commune feeling about us – you've picked up the vibe already, I can tell – and then we've got Nick and Bobby."

"Not the drummer – Leo – and the rest of the band?"

"Nah. They're okay guys, sure, but Nick's the brains of this lot, and Bobby's the heart."

"And you?"

Pig grinned. "Just strong muscle when needed." He looked around over the room, almost paternally, Leo thought. "Yeah, time we crashed." He called over to one of the other Rabbits, sprawled on the floor, one tattooed arm around a female Rabbit's waist, and the other clutching a can. "Oi! Letch! Have the Others packed up the PA and got it stashed yet?"

"Absolutely no problem, Pig. All present and correct, sir." He spoke in what might have been an outrageous parody of an upper-class Oxford accent, but Leo had a suspicion that it might not actually be a parody.

"OK, gang." Pig raised his voice. "We've had your glasses, now let's see your arses. Time for bed, boys and girls."

There was surprisingly little dissent as the group picked up their beer cans and other rubbish, and placed it neatly into bin-liners marked with the appropriate recycling labels. Leo watched in astonishment, which

Pig noticed.

"Yeah, not your usual gang of roughneck roadies, are they? Come with me." Pig led the way to the car park outside the Hall, and pointed to a large yellow double-decker bus with "KILLER RABBITS" in large red letters down the side. "You're upstairs. 17A. Your shit is all on the bunk." Bunk? Leo wondered to himself. "The women sleep downstairs. Off-limits. Unisex showers and toilets downstairs as well. Don't break your neck going down the stairs for a piss in the middle of the night. Sleep well." And he was off into the night.

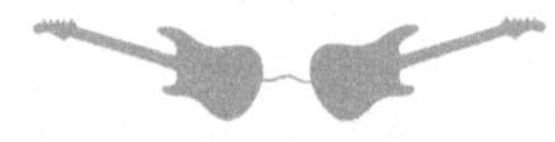

Chapter 7

The top floor of the Rabbit Hutch (as Leo found its inhabitants had named the bus), had been efficiently converted into sleeping quarters, with two-tier bunks like those in train sleeping cars. The atmosphere was quieter and less boisterous than Leo remembered the communal living at Scout camps and the like to have been. The men got themselves ready for bed in their own individual ways. Some appeared to sleep wearing all their daytime clothes, some stripped down to underwear, and a few went all the way and changed into pyjamas.

Leo's things were on the top bunk, neatly packed in a gym bag he remembered buying once when he had thought he might buy a gym membership to go with it. He chose the halfway path of underwear, after checking the contents of the bag.

The main lights went out, and one by one, the individual berth lights were turned off. Some voices from the darkness.

"Where is it tomorrow?"

"Brighton."

"Bloody Brighton."

"It's not too bad. And after that?"

"We spend a couple of days getting ready for Japan."

"Fucking Japan. That new guy's going to take us round there, isn't he? Crane?"

"Yeah. Crane, you there?"

The bus started off with a lurch, and despite himself, Leo gave a little startled cry.

"OK, mate," said his neighbour across the aisle in a quiet, soft voice. "There's a belt like an airline safety belt you can fasten to strap yourself in. Curly's a good driver, though. He won't spill you out."

"Crane, you there?" the voice repeated.

"I'm here," he said, fumbling for the belt.

"What's Japan like?"

"How do you mean?"

"Do they speak English? In the shops and that, I mean?"

"Some do, but not a lot. And it's funny English sometimes."

"But you speak Japanese, right?"

"Yes," Leo admitted.

"Clever guy," came another voice. "Hear that Nick found you this morning? What happened?"

Without meaning to, Leo found himself telling how he had left Gail that morning, and gone round to Sharon's, and what had happened there. There was silence from the others as he related his story, the bus sighing around corners, and stopping and starting at traffic lights. The yellow glare of sodium street-lights flared through gaps in the curtains as the bus made its way through the suburban streets before they reached the motorway and started a steady drone southwards.

"Sounds like you're well out of that mess, mate," said a new voice. "Make a new start with the Rabbits."

"Sounds like Nick picked a right one this time," said another, and there was laughter, though it was friendly and not mocking.

"You're okay with us, you know," said the voice that had told him about the safety belt. "We're the good guys."

"Yeah, angels, all of us," and there was more laughter, and murmurs of agreement.

What the hell was all this? Leo asked himself. Who were these people? It sure as hell wasn't your average rock band.

"He did all right tonight with Bobby," came a voice that Leo recognised as that of Chaz.

"Yeah, Pig said so," said another.

"Good on you, Froo," said an Australian twang.

"Froo? Who the fuck is Froo?" asked another. "Is that another of your stupid Aussie convict words?"

"Nah. He's Froo, right? Well, what's it say on the back of the trucks?"

"Crane Fruehauf," someone said after a while.

"Yeah, well, that's a bit long, so he's Froo now. That okay with you, Froo?"

"Do I have a choice?" Leo asked, and laughed.

"That's the right spirit, mate."

"When are you buggers going to shut up and get some sleep?" came a voice that sounded like Scuzz.

"Okay, 'night all."

The bus sped on, and the upper deck gradually filled with the sounds of snoring. Leo lay awake, wondering exactly what kind of lunatic asylum he had entered, until the roar of the bus and the gentle swaying rocked him to sleep.

He awoke, as did everyone else, to the sound of a klaxon and Pig's roar from below. "All right, you lazy bastards! It's eight o'clock, and time you were all awake."

Somehow, sixteen men and four women managed to struggle awake and get themselves prepared for the day with the limited facilities available in the bus.

"Sleep well, Crane?" Pig asked, almost kindly, as Leo staggered off the bus.

"He's Froo now," an eavesdropper said, and explained.

"Okay, Froo it is, then. Told you your name would change. How do you feel?"

"Fine."

"She's good, isn't she?" Pig said with a touch of pride, jerking his thumb towards the bus. "My own design. And the only fucking time in my life that I've ever used fluid mechanics in a practical application. I redesigned the suspension system."

"It works pretty well," Leo admitted.

"Band will come up in a bit," Pig said. "Grab yourself some breakfast over there – we don't eat Indian at breakfast unless you really want to – and then you've got to go shopping."

"Eh?"

"Bobby said she wanted some new guitar straps, right? Make sure you get something comfortable. Nothing but skin and bone, that one, and most straps dig in something cruel. Unless you want to spend all night rubbing her back?" Pig looked at Leo and laughed. "Aha, she's got you by the short and curlies, has she? Takes all sorts, I guess."

"You're not one of those who can read minds, then?"

"Not a bloody chance. I just read faces. Now bugger

off and get some breakfast. Here, use these to pay for the straps." Pig handed him a wad of ten-pound notes.

There was a fairly conventional breakfast buffet set up in one of the backstage rooms. While picking up some yogurt and cereal and a couple of croissants (he passed on the bacon and black pudding sandwiches), Leo discovered that they were at the Brighton Dome, and the Others, as the Rabbits referred to the temporary fetchers and carriers, were already at work setting up the speaker stacks.

"How big is the audience here?" he asked Chaz.

"Couple of thousand, tops."

"Not that many," said another Rabbit. Leo recognised him as Duck, the one he had embarrassingly mistaken for Sharon the day before. "Fifteen hundred or so."

"Why do you play such small places, when the other big names play the arenas and the really enormous places?" asked Leo.

"Because they're barking mad," said another passing Rabbit, who introduced himself as Keef. "They say they don't want the stadiums. And they sell enough albums that they can get away with saying that sort of thing."

"Good for them," said Duck.

"But all this," Leo waved his hand at the assembled Rabbits, "and the bus and all the rest of it. This doesn't all come from record royalties, does it? You're not telling me the tickets are paying for all this?"

"It's not all tickets," said Duck. "There's the souvenir T-shirts."

"And the posters, said Chaz.

"And the baseball caps," said Keef.

"And… Well, we'll let Pig tell you about the other, I reckon. Maybe best if he explains it."

God, these people were seriously weird. He wasn't even sure that this was something he wanted to get mixed up in. Was it criminal? he asked himself, and then was reminded that he was a fine one to talk, having removed three million pounds of other people's money into a Japanese bank.

"How did you join the Rabbits?" he asked them. It was Duck who answered.

"I've got my Master's in late medieval history. Bloody useless subject, really, but it was quite fun to do. Loved the Plantagenets, hated the Tudors. Ended up getting about the only job that really fitted that sort of thing. Curator of medieval antiquities at a museum in the Midlands. Some rather valuable church plate, chalices and the rest of the stuff that had somehow survived the Reformation and Cromwell, went missing one day. So did I. I met Nick."

"Ah," said Leo. This was beginning to sound familiar.

"Nick just sort of knows what's going on with people," Duck said. "So I became a Rabbit."

"Me, it was just money out of the supermarket tills where I was assistant manager," said Chaz. "Mind you, I say 'just', but it ended up being quite a lot when I added it all up. Mind you, once I had it, I wasn't sure what to do about it all. And I met Nick, and then became a Rabbit."

"Bloody hell. You're all—" He wasn't sure what word was appropriate.

"Yes, we are," grinned Chaz. "And so are you, if Nick's right."

"I thought he was saying it as a joke," Leo complained.

"Oh, Nick never jokes," said Keef. "Except when he does. So three million nicker, eh? Want to tell us about it?"

"Not now. I will, though. Some time in the future. What about Scuzz, what's he done?"

"He was in the Passport Office. What do you think?"

Leo thought. "Got it. Pig?"

The others' faces went blank. "Can't say," Chaz said at length. "If you really want to know, ask him yourself, but I don't think he'll be happy if you do. You'll have to wait for the right moment."

"Which is never," Duck said.

"Never," Keef agreed.

"So don't ask him?"

"Right."

Somehow it seemed natural to be sitting round on folding chairs in the backstage area of a concert hall, spooning yoghurt and muesli out of disposable bowls, and talking with friends about how much money they had stolen from different institutions.

"I could get used to this sort of life," he said, pouring himself a second cup of excellent coffee.

"You don't really have a lot of choice," said Keef. "You don't leave the Rabbits, you know."

"But it can't suit everyone," said Leo.

"Well, that's true," said Chaz. "You could always try being an undertaker in the Isle of Man."

"Or buggering off to Australia," said Duck.

"Or—" said Keef, drawing the edge of his hand across his throat.

"And all those are if Pig doesn't get to me first, I suppose?"

"You're a smart one, Froo. You'll do all right with the Rabbits."

Leo sipped his coffee. It seemed that there were some special skills needed to survive in this strange environment. "I've got to do some shopping," he said, standing up and finishing his coffee. "Anyone know where there's a music shop around here? Guitar straps for Bobby."

No-one knew where to go, so he wandered into town, and asked passers-by for the best guitar shop in town. It took him five shops before he found straps that he thought Bobby would appreciate. Asking for eight identical guitar straps raised some eyebrows behind the counter, but he got the straps and returned back to the Dome. Everyone else had eaten lunch, but he'd grabbed a sandwich in town.

He was pleased that Bobby seemed pleased with his purchases, but she was somewhat offhand, compared to her mood of the previous night.

"No need to fuss over me," she said, almost snapping at him at one point. "I'm not a doll, and I can take care of myself." He had just fetched her a fleece top and attempted to drape it around her shoulders after she had complained of being a little cold. "Oh, don't be offended, for God's sake," she said. "It's just that I get in these moods sometimes, and there's not a lot you or anyone else can do about them. It'll go in an hour or so. You've done really well with those straps, if it makes you feel any better. They're just what I'd have chosen for myself. So well done, and now bugger off and leave me to myself. Knock on my door in a couple of hours and come and talk to me if I tell you to come in. If I don't want you to come in, I'll tell you to fuck off." She smiled, and there was no malice or hostility in her face.

"Fine." Leo forced a smile back, though he was disappointed not to be spending more time with Bobby, who seemed to be rapidly becoming an obsession.

He ran into Chaz as he walked along the corridor. "Not a lot for us to do for a bit," said Chaz. "Come on, let's walk down to the beach and throw bits of bread to seagulls or roll up our trouser legs and paddle in the sea or something."

They went down to the beach, but the wind was too cold for Leo to think of paddling, though Chaz made an exploratory dip of his bare feet into the sea, and came running out yelping when the first wave soaked him above the knee.

"Daft bugger," said Leo, laughing.

"Yeah, we're all daft," said Chaz. "And you think we're either crooked as knotted corkscrews or out of our tiny little minds, right? Maybe a bit of both?"

"I wouldn't put it quite that way," said Leo. "But yes and yes and yes."

"I can't tell you what we actually do," said Chaz. "That's Pig's job, not mine. We're not just a band on tour, as you must have worked out. But believe me, we are on the side of the angels. Yeah, I told you what I did, nicking the money out of the tills at the supermarket and fiddling the accounts. And you've told me what you did. But now, it's different. If you stick with the Rabbits, Crane or Froo or whatever stupid name you have right now, believe me, you're in for the ride of your life. You're going to have a lot of fun, and I mean a lot. And what's so good about that, is you're going to feel good inside yourself about it."

Chaz said all this with a look of complete sincerity on his face. It was the sort of look that Leo had seen on the faces of evangelical religious converts.

"Look, this isn't to do with God and religion and the rest of that crap, is it? Because if it is, and it sounds like it from the way you're talking that it is, I'm out of here. I like you and the rest of the Rabbits, and I—" He broke off, realising that he didn't want to discuss his feelings for Bobby with anyone at the moment.

Chaz laughed. "It's not religion, I promise you. Sure, we've got some Rabbits who you might call believers, and some who don't believe in anything up there, and probably some who believe in some really weird shit, but it's not something we talk about. No-one's going to persuade you to join a cult and give your life to Jesus, or sacrifice babies at full moon. I think Jesus and the Buddha and the rest of them might like what we're doing, mind, but that's not why we're doing it."

"And you can't say what 'it' is?"

"More than my job's worth, mate." Chaz shook his head, and then looked at his watch. "Time we were getting back. Set up the guitars in a minute."

"And then I promised to go and see Bobby."

"Yeah. Takes some looking after, that one, but Bobby's not too bad, right?"

"She's fine." Leo realised that he had given away Bobby's secret to Chaz without meaning to do it, even if Chaz might have guessed the previous night that he knew.

Chaz grinned at him. "So you found out for sure, did you? Good for you." He said no more about the subject, for which Leo was grateful.

They returned to the Dome, and went on stage to start getting the guitars ready. Before he had completely finished setting up, Leo realised that it was time to go and see Bobby, and he set off to see her. Although she asked him to come in when he knocked on the door, it didn't seem that she really wanted to talk to him at all. She was sitting there with her head in her hands, moaning softly to herself.

"I really don't know if I can go on tonight," she said. "It's just going to be too much for me."

Leo's instinct was to put his arm round her and hug

her, but he knew this was not what she wanted, and he refrained from touching her. "Is there anything I can do?" he asked, feeling completely useless.

"Not a lot really, but thank you for asking anyway," she replied in a voice which was so quiet that he could hardly hear it. "Just sit down on that chair over there and keep quiet. It's just nice for me to know that there's someone else in the room."

Thirty minutes of sitting quietly later, Leo was bored out of his skull. Bobby had hardly moved in that time, except to shift her position slightly. Suddenly she looked up. "Go and look for Nick, would you, please, dear?"

Leo was relieved to be able to do something other than just sit there. He left the room, and found the dressing room with Nick's name written on the door. He knocked.

"Bobby is just sitting there and says that she can't go on stage tonight," he told Nick when the door opened.

"And I suppose she's not telling you why?"

"She says it will be too much for her, whatever that means."

"Oh Christ. Here we go again." Nick sighed, but it did not seem like an angry sound. "This is something for me and not for you. If you've got anything that you have to do on stage, go ahead and do it. I'll make sure that you are called if she asks for you or anything."

Leo had mixed emotions as he returned to the stage and continued setting up the guitars and testing them with the effects. One of those times of the month? he asked himself. He wasn't really sure. Despite having been married for several years, and having had his fair share of girlfriends over the years, some female mysteries still eluded his understanding.

He'd just finished setting up and testing the guitar that

she used on "Ladder", his final task in the setup procedure, when one of the female Rabbits called to him from the side of the stage. "Hey, Froo, Bobby wants you soon as you're ready."

"Coming," he called back. "I'm through here, Chaz. See you in a bit."

"Sorry I was so bitchy just now," she said as he entered her dressing room. "You probably think I'm on junk or something like that, and I need a fix. Well, it's a lot more complicated than that, and it's a matter of running away from the fix rather than wanting one. You'll understand a lot more once Pig has talked to you."

"Everyone says that I'm going to understand when he talks to me," Leo complained, "but I've no idea when that's going to be."

"It'll be when the time is right. Done the guitars? New straps and everything?" He nodded. "Great, well done. Now, what am I going to wear tonight on stage? Have a look at what's on the hangers over there and tell me what you think would look good tonight."

"I thought you looked pretty good last night in the leather."

"Sure, but I was sweating like a pig under the lights. Just put your nose inside that jacket and sniff."

He did, and it smelt wonderful to him. Yes, there was a smell of stale sweat, but there was also the feminine musky smell that he had always associated with his first ever girlfriend, and which he had hardly ever experienced since then.

"You are truly fucking weird," she said. "You seem to get off on the sound of me peeing and on the smell of my sweat and on the fact I don't shave my armpits all that often – yes, I could tell that you were looking yesterday. I suppose I should be flattered, because they're not the kind of things that most men look for in a girl, and it's always nice to be appreciated, but it doesn't mean to say you're normal."

"Are you using your telepathy or whatever it is?" Leo said. "I don't like being eavesdropped on in that sort of way."

"Can't turn it off, darling. Sometimes wish I could. In fact, that was most of the problem just then. Tonight, there are going to be fifteen hundred screaming egos out there, and I've got to listen to them all, whether I want to or not. I don't have a choice in the matter. It's like having your eyes open all the time and not being able to close them. You just can't help seeing what's round you all the time, and taking notice of it."

"Sorry," said Leo. "I'd always thought it was a good thing to have those sort of superpowers."

"Don't say things like that!" she flashed at him. "You make me and Nick sound like a couple of freaks." She took a drink from a bottle of mineral water standing in front of her, and it seemed to calm her a little. "I guess it is a good thing some of the time. It's the reason why Nick and I sound so good when we're playing together, of course, and we are good, you know."

Leo saw his cue. "The encore last night was pure magic. Really great."

"Of course I know how you felt about it." She smiled, as if the memory gave her pleasure. "Nick and I, we can just sync up like that, and yeah, magic. I suppose it is magic. We'd have been burned as witches or magicians in the old days, I guess. Now we're just musicians, right?"

She spread her hands on her legs and flexed her fingers. Long, sensitive, fingers, drumming on her thighs. Leo started to imagine those fingers stroking their way across his skin, closer and closer to—

"Stop that now." There was a snap in her voice. "I don't mind you having fantasies, but I'm rehearsing, and you're distracting me. If you can't think about anything except trying to get me into bed, you're going to have to find another job in the Rabbits."

"Sorry," he said. "Got anything to read?"

"There's a *Guardian* in the waste-paper bin. See if you can finish the crossword."

He was somewhat amazed to find that there were only a few clues left to fill in. Someone, either Bobby or Nick, or both, had filled in most of the crossword.

"It's 'terracotta' on 7 across," he said to her, after a few minutes. She had her eyes closed.

"Shush," she said, and carried on moving her fingers. The irritation seemed to have left her voice, though. He went back to 3 down. "Ephemeral," he said.

"I thought it was," she said, opening her eyes. "Nick didn't believe me. Thank you. Bring it over here. I'm done with the practice."

They sat together finishing the crossword, which, when he thought about it, was something he'd never even done with Gail. It all seemed ridiculously domestic, though they were sitting in a theatre dressing-room, perched together on the edge of the daybed, heads together over the paper.

"Yeah, we make an odd couple, don't we?" She laughed. "You're going to have to get used to this, you know, if we're going to stay together."

"Are we?"

"Oh, I hope so. Once you can get over your crazy urges to jump me. They make me nervous, even though I know you're not going to do anything about them."

There's one way to stop them, Leo thought to himself.

"And it's not going to happen," she told him. "Not for a bit, anyway. You're too jangled. Your nerves are a mess. If we went to bed, you wouldn't know who you were fucking. Me, your wife, the other one, whoever. Cool down, take time, sort yourself out. And then we'll see, right?"

It wasn't exactly a promise, but it was better than nothing.

Pig's voice echoed down the corridor, informing the world that the evening meal was ready. "Off you go, then," she said. "Come back and get me ready. Thanks."

Aubergine and potato curry, and a fish curry with coconut and cashews, with saffron rice. Again, excellent. The atmosphere was the same as before. Everyone ate in silence, which he now recognised as concentration, and at the end of the meal, the same chant and encouragement from Pig. And he still didn't know what was really happening. The rock band was only a part of it, obviously.

As he left the room to go back to Bobby, he heard Pig ask someone, "Are the Others out of the way now? Can we move the Feelers in?" The capital letters were almost audible.

"Hey, Chaz," he called as soon as he was round the corner and out of earshot (he hoped) of Pig. "Who are the Others?" He thought he understood the jargon, but he wanted to make sure.

"Oh, just the ones who aren't Rabbits. The ones who do the heavy lifting and setting up and tearing down the PA. Local hire companies, usually. Long on muscle, short on brains."

"And the Feelers?"

The grin left Chaz' face. "That's for Pig to tell you,

not me."

Damn it. This was frustrating. Doubly frustrating, he thought, as he entered Bobby's dressing-room, and saw her sitting there in her white T-shirt.

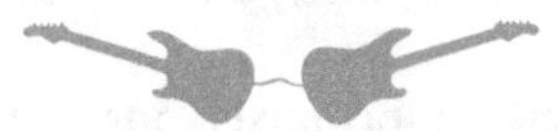

Chapter 8

"It's the leather rig again tonight," she told him. "You're right, it looks good, and it suits my mood tonight."

"You're okay?" getting the trousers, and taking her jeans from her.

"I'm fine. Thanks for asking, though." She stripped off the T-shirt. "Bra, please." She turned her back for him to undo her bra.

Obediently he undid the hooks. Getting quite good at this, he thought, deliberately concentrating on the bra rather than on whatever it was covering.

"Great. Well done. You didn't pinch me like you did last night."

"Sorry, I didn't realise I'd done that. You should have said."

"Didn't hurt much. Not worth making a fuss over. I've suffered worse in my time. And you're learning to straighten out your mind. Well done."

Leo resented being talked to as though he was a small boy, but he appreciated that he was behaving like one a lot of the time, especially around her.

"There," she said, when she was in full battledress. "Looking good?"

"Looking good," he confirmed.

"Now, let's do that breathing thing we did yesterday. Okay?" He faced her, and she took his hands, and they closed their eyes. Breathing together. In. Out. In. Out. In. Out.

"That was pretty magic," he said, after she had dropped his hands and he had opened his eyes. "I don't know what you were doing, but it was something pretty special."

"Not me," she said, shaking her head. "That's you doing it. Well done. Feel better?"

"Yeah."

"So do I."

"What is that breathing thing?"

"I read about it somewhere. I think it was an Aztec or an Inca thing, according to the book. Which, of course, is crap, but it sounded interesting, and I tried it with a few people, and it does do something, doesn't it?"

"Not sure what, but yes, it does."

"Okay, thanks. See you on stage. Off you go."

The gig went well. The fans were enthusiastic, and "Ladder" was the encore again. Once more, Bobby played around the tune, weaving complex melodies around the well-known theme that had been recorded so many years before, and Leo felt she was playing to him and every other man in the hall. But then, he told himself, he knew something about Bobby that the rest of the world didn't. At the end of the number, the audience erupted, and Leo started applauding with the rest, almost missing the guitar Bobby threw at him as she stalked off-stage.

"That was magic," he said to Chaz, as they packed

up the guitars.

"Yeah, magic," Chaz said. "I've heard them play that more times than I can count, but that's the best ever. She's something else, isn't she? I reckon you must be good for her."

"Hah," was the only answer that Leo could think of.

"Done?" Chaz called out after a few minutes. "Beer time."

They trooped off, and grabbed their cans of beer. Pig was sitting in the same corner as before, and beckoned Leo over.

"You're doing good," were his first words to Leo. "I'm going to need you for the next day or so, if you can tear yourself away from Bobby. Reckon you can do that?"

"I guess so. What do you need me for?"

"We're off to Japan in a few days, as you know, and there's a shitload of papers. We're not playing any more gigs until we go, so I want you to look over some of the crap. Hotel bookings, that sort of thing. Promoters' contracts, maybe, but we've had lawyers at both ends look over them, so there shouldn't be too much of that. Sound good to you?"

"You're asking me as if I had a choice."

"Just being polite, that's all. I can manage it sometimes." Pig grinned. "And then I'm going to want you to sit with me on the flight. It's a privilege, believe me. You get to fly business class. Nick and Bobby and the rest of them go first, I go business, mainly because I don't fit into an economy, and the rest go that class between economy and business where you get a bit more legroom and some better food. But the flight's going to be when you find out what the Rabbits are really all about. I think you're going to like it. And then I'm going to need your help again."

"When we get to Tokyo, you mean? Help as a tour guide and so on?"

"That, yes, but there's more. I'll explain on the plane."

"OK." Leo was torn up with curiosity about what Pig wanted to tell him, and why he wanted to tell him while they were over the middle of the Siberian tundra. He guessed that there was no way to run away on a plane, and any kind of fight or argument would be quickly stopped by the flight attendants. All in all, if you had a difficult interview to give, then a plane was probably one of the best places to give it.

The night was spent in the Rabbit Hutch, which took them to a Georgian country house lived in by, Leo discovered when he asked, a relative of Letch's, the Rabbit who had answered Leo's question about the Others, and seemed to be in charge of such things. According to Chaz and Duck, the house actually belonged to Letch, who was, according to them, officially Lord Somebody, the younger son of one of England's biggest landowners, and it had been christened the Permanent Rabbit Hutch by the Rabbits.

"A very useful Rabbit to have on your side," Duck remarked. "This is our base when we're not touring."

"A sort of mini-stately home from home," said Chaz. "We sleep in the Hutch, still, but we can use the house in the daytime."

As Pig had promised, there was a lot of paperwork. Pig proved to have a very sharp head when it came to the details of the tour, and the questions he asked stretched Leo to the limit. Leo found himself over his head with the Japanese legal language at one point, and had to resort to an online dictionary. Even so, Pig was pleased.

"This tour's going to cost a lot of money," Leo said at one point.

Pig said nothing, but nodded.

"Is it going to make money? I don't see how it can, looking at these figures."

"It's not," Pig confirmed.

"So you're going to make it up on the CDs and the T-shirts and the baseball caps and the rest of the shit?"

"No."

"But you're not doing this as a charity event. So what the hell?"

Pig stroked his beard. "You're right, the tour's not going to make money. But at the same time, the Rabbits are going to be at least three million dollars better off leaving Japan than when they entered. And that's not counting the part of the three million pounds of yours waiting for you over there that you're going to give us."

"Am I?"

"I think you will want to, once you've heard what I have to tell you on the plane."

There it was again – "on the plane". Why the hell couldn't he be told now, in a normal setting, instead of 30,000 feet over Omsk? And what kind of thing would make him want to give away that sort of money?

He found it hard to concentrate on the rest of the preparations, but at last Pig called an end to the work. They'd been at it for almost two solid days, and Leo felt his eyes were blurred, and his head felt it would explode from sensory overload. He leaned back in the desk chair and stretched, groaning.

Pig grinned. "Yeah, it's been a long couple of days. If I'd known it was going to be this much work, I'd have made it three, and not two. You did good, though. Now go and have a walk round the grounds or go swimming or something."

"Swim? Where?" Swimming was actually one of the few forms of exercise that Leo actually enjoyed.

"There's a pool in one of the greenhouses."

"Sounds good."

He took himself outside, and walked around the outside of the house to the back, where he found the greenhouses, looking like miniature versions of the ones at Kew Gardens. One of them had indeed been converted to a swimming-pool. He entered the greenhouse, and his footsteps echoed in the empty space. It was indeed empty, he discovered. No-one swimming, and the row of cubicles showed no sign of occupation. He had no swimming trunks, and he considered leaving his underpants on in the interests of in the interests of what? Damn it. He stripped, and decided to shower before entering the water, feeling somewhat dirty and sweaty after the long haul with Pig through the paperwork.

A few minutes later he was swimming lengths and feeling good in himself. After a little while the swimming turned into a routine, and he started to daydream. He started thinking about what on earth Pig was going to tell him. Six lengths. Was it some sort of religious cult? He didn't think so, and he'd been told it wasn't. Seven lengths. Or was it a question of something criminal? But they all seemed to believe they were on the side of the angels. Eight. And then he turned to more personal things. He persuaded himself that yes, he'd made the right decision to leave Gail, and that he was now free. Nine lengths. And Sharon was a bitch and he was going to have nothing more to do with her. Ten. And he wasn't really interested in Bobby. Really. Eleven. And then he started swimming again. Fifteen lengths seemed to be enough. He lay on his back and floated. His ears were underwater, and he could hear nothing as he drift-ed peacefully. Could you go to sleep while you were floating? he wondered. He felt himself drifting off.

Without warning, he jerked fully alert as a hand closed around his ankle. He sat up, sank, swallowed water, surfaced, spat out the water, and wiped his eyes. He had drifted to the edge, and Bobby was standing by the side of the pool, smiling. She was naked.

"Good," she said. "I didn't think you were dead, but I wanted to make sure. Sorry to have startled you like that. Were you asleep?"

"Yes. No. Sort of." He looked away, conscious of his own nakedness and her eyes fixed on his groin.

"Oh, look if you want to," she said. "I wouldn't have come to see you if I minded. Here." She turned slowly, giving him a look at her naked body from all sides.

"You're beautiful," he said, and meant it. He hadn't meant to say that, but it had just slipped out. She was, too, in the way that a samurai sword, or a nuclear sub-marine, or a well-designed fighter plane, or some such fast and deadly object is beautiful. Nothing wasted, nothing spare, and lines that might have come from a draughtsman's drawing board. Even the sparse black tuft between her legs didn't break the flow.

"Thanks," she said. "You didn't have to say it, but thanks." Suddenly, she was in the water beside him. "You been busy with Pig?" she called, as she breast-stroked her way to the other end of the pool. "Come on, come and swim beside me, or are you too tired?"

"Yes, tired. I've been with Pig. Sorting out all the things for Japan." He'd caught up with her by this time, and he glanced over. Her dark mane of hair hung in rat-tails over that perfect neck, and as she swam, her curves rose and fell tantalisingly in and out of view.

He was all too conscious of her femininity, and he stopped swimming and started to float again. He started to turn over on his back, and then realised he was nude, with the common reaction of a man to an attractive woman, and decided to stay face-down.

"You all right there?" she called, and looked in his direction with the expression that he guessed meant she was somehow reading his emotions or whatever it was that she did. "Oh. I'm sorry. I've really screwed you up, haven't I? Maybe it's time we did something about it at last. Come on," and she swam for the ladder at the edge of the pool and climbed out.

He followed, holding his hands in front of his groin.

"Here," she said, throwing a towel in his direction. She was already wrapped in another towel from the pile beside the cubicles. "Dry yourself with this, and bring another three or four, and meet me over there." She pointed to a grove of large potted plants on the other side of the pool.

Dumbly, he dried himself off, and, towel knotted around his waist, picked up some clean towels, and joined Bobby, who was standing by a sun-bed, screened on three sides by the plants. No-one could see them from the pool, and the greenhouse windows at this place looked onto a blank wall. Her towel was on the floor by her feet, and she stood facing him. She seemed to be completely unselfconscious.

"Spread those towels over there on the sun-bed and then let's do the breathing thing again. Come on, face me, hold my hands, and close your eyes."

Once more, they started their breathing together. In. Out. In. Out. At least fifty times, he reckoned.

"That's wonderful. Now we're really in sync. Take off your towel and lie there on your back. Lift your knees a bit and open your legs a little. I'm not going to hurt you. Don't be shy." Dumbly, he obeyed. "Now before we start, have you got any nasty diseases?" Again that expression. "Well, you don't seem to think you have, so we'll take that as a no, shall we?"

She sat beside him on the edge of the sun-bed, and her long guitarist's fingers stroked one thigh. "Don't speak," she told him. "It's fun for me to discover what you like without you saying anything to me. Close your eyes. No, keep your hands off me for now," as his hands reached up to where he imagined her small breasts to be. "Later." A gentle slap on his stomach.

He could feel two hands now. They traced their way slowly up his body to his nipples, and then down again, taking a slightly different route, down the centre, past his navel, and carrying on down to what had now become the focus of his entire being. "Keep your eyes closed," she told him. The fingers fluttered over his groin, and he felt he was going to explode there and then. "Not yet," she warned him, and the fingers went away.

"Hope this is going to take the weight of both of us," she said, and he could feel her getting onto the sun-bed, which creaked and swayed, but held up. Her legs straddled his body as she knelt over him. "Now you can start using your hands," she told him. "Keep your eyes closed and explore. See me with your fingertips. Start at my back."

He traced a path from her waist up the delicate knobs of her spine, covered with the soft downy hair he had noticed, and ran his fingers below her hairline, to her smooth firm neck. Her skin shivered at his touch on her neck and on her shoulders, and as his hands continued to move down her chest. The nipples at the end of the small breasts were hard, and he squeezed them.

"Gently, gently," she warned him. "I'm not into pain. Just hold me there."

As he cupped her breasts in his palms, he could feel her moving over his body, and suddenly, without warning, he was inside her with almost no resistance as she slipped herself around him. Her hands rested on his shoulders as she moved back and forth to a rhythm of her own making. He tried to match it and failed. "Shush…" she said, and a hand came off his shoulder, and a finger was laid across his lips. "I'm the musician, remember? Just lie back and enjoy the ride."

He came after what seemed like hours of being brought to the brink and being held back, suddenly and explosively, and at the same time he could feel her contracting as she let out a low moan, like nothing he'd ever heard before from any woman.

There was silence for a minute as neither of them moved. She broke the silence. "That was pretty damn good, don't you think? You can open your eyes, by the way." He did, and watched her swing one leg over him, get off the sun-bed, and stand up.

"That was amazing," he said. "If that's what your not-telepathy does for you…"

"I have a feeling that you might start to be able to do the same thing," she said, picking up the towel and draping it around her. "I'd like to work on you and develop your talent that way." And without another word, she went off, and he heard the shower start up.

He lay there, wondering what exactly had happened. Had he been used or had something more happened just then? And what did she mean about him possibly having that strange ability? The noise of the shower stopped. He picked up the towels and made his way to the shower, soaped and rinsed, and dressed, hearing the door to the greenhouse open and shut as he pulled the Rabbits T-shirt over his head.

As he thought, she had gone while he was dressing.

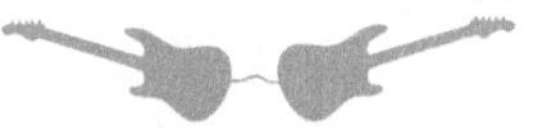

Chapter 9

Leo walked back to the house from the greenhouse. He was glad that he didn't meet anyone on the way. He wanted the time to himself. What had Bobby meant when she had said that he might possess some of the same powers that she did? The question preyed on his mind even more than what he had just enjoyed. And he had enjoyed it, he told himself, as much as he ever had. There was something about Bobby that really did make it special.

As soon as he walked through the door of the house, Pig grabbed him to help with the shippers who were transporting the band gear to Japan, a day in advance of the band and the Rabbits were to fly there.

"Reckon working in a bank helps you understand some of this shit," said Pig, waving a few sheets of legalese which Leo had untangled, and pronounced as a mass of meaningless gobbledegook, much to the shippers' disgust. "You just saved us wasting a couple of grand on a crappy meaningless insurance policy. Well done. You earned your keep this week at least."

Leo smiled reflexively. There were other rewards over

and above just his keep, he felt, and he'd already had the first instalment of them. He hoped it wouldn't be the last one.

He remained wrapped up in his own world for the rest of the evening, but as if he'd hung a "Do Not Disturb" sign round his neck, no-one bothered him, for which he was very thankful.

"Off to catch the plane tomorrow," said Chaz as they got ready for bed in the Rabbit Hutch. "And then Tokyo. Home from home for you, Froo?"

"Hardly," said Leo. "Been there a few times, but it's hardly home."

"But you know your way around, right? You'll be able to show us some of the sights, right?"

"Sure. Whatever." Chaz sensed that he wasn't in a mood to chat, and to Leo's relief stopped talking.

The next day reminded Leo of why he hated going on group package tours, which had been Gail's favourite form of vacation. Endless lines everywhere. From getting the baggage trolleys, the security lines, everything seemed to take twice as long as it would if he was travelling on his own. Happily, since he was flying business class, the line to check in and to get on the plane was not as long as it was for the rest of the Rabbits, who shot envious glances in his and Pig's direction.

The Belgian passport that Scuzz had provided raised no official eyebrows, much to his relief, and he settled into his seat, and gratefully accepted the complimentary champagne and snacks.

"Don't imagine you're going to travel like this on every tour," Pig growled to him from the next seat. To Leo's amusement, Pig was travelling with a Danish passport. To his amusement, because he had no difficulty in imagining him in a horned helmet, storming ashore from a longboat at the head of a gang of looting, pillaging and raping Vikings.

"I won't. But it's nice once in a while."

Once they were safely airborne, and the meal had been served and cleared away, Pig turned to Leo.

"OK. Now it's time. Time you learned what the Rabbits are all about. As you have guessed, we are a band, and a bloody good one. Nick and Bobby can bring tears to your eyes when they play well, which is most of the time. We're a pretty good road crew, as well, as you can see. But...?" He let the sentence hang in the air as a question.

"You're all too well-educated and too intelligent to be roadies," said Leo.

"Glad you make a distinction between the two – education and intelligence," said Pig. "Lot of people confuse the two. The fact that you don't is a sign of the second. But yeah, right. We're too damn smart to be breaking our backs lugging speaker stacks around. Even with all the computers and shit that passes for audio gear now, yeah. We're too smart." He called the attendant and ordered a couple of Bloody Marys. "Best thing for flying," he said. "Replaces salt loss, and the vitamins help with jet-lag."

"And the vodka?"

"Helps you forget you're stuck in a tin tube held up by faith and magic. Okay, so what do we do? Nick and Bobby have this gift. I'm sure Bobby's told you by now, hasn't she?" His voice had dropped to a low rumble, and Leo had to strain to hear him over the noise of the plane.

"You mean about feeling other people's emotions? Yeah, she told me that. And that Nick had it, too."

"I guess everyone's got a bit of that about them," said

Pig ruminatively, "except most people are scared of it and don't want to use it. These two, though, they're good. Now Nick, as well as being one of these super-sensitive types, is nobody's fool. He can feel the vibes coming off the audience when he plays, and of course that's one of the reasons why he's so good and the fans love him. He plays back to them what they want to hear."

"Bobby too?"

"This part of the story's about Nick. We'll get to Bobby in a little bit. Nick thinks he can use this gift of his somehow. But how? He now knows how the audience – several thousand fans with money to spend – think."

"Sell the data to a market research firm?"

"You're on the right track. Trouble is that it's not data. It's just a stream of impressions in Nick's head. He's smart, he's got a good memory, but this is two thousand people we're talking about, right? And the thing is, he's playing his arse off while he's picking all this up. With the best will in the world, you can't call this 'data', can you?"

"Good point."

"Well, Nick's smart, but he doesn't have the technical chops, so he calls me in – we grew up nearly next door to each other, and he knew me when I was a little skinny kid," Pig grinned, "and I knew him when he was a littler skinnier kid. I went to uni, and carried on from there after my degree. He became a muso. But we stayed in touch, and so when he wanted help, Nick got in touch with me."

"What did he want?"

"He wanted a way to record the things he was picking up from the audience."

"That's impossible!" said Leo. "There's no way that telepathy, or whatever it is that he and Bobby do, is physical, and so you can't even start about thinking recording it on a computer or whatever."

Pig shook his head. "You're not understanding me. What Nick wanted was not a way of recording the thoughts and impressions he was picking up – he wanted to record his reactions to those thoughts. Now that's brainwaves and brain patterns, and you can actually record those as data. Interpreting them is a bitch, though."

"I'm beginning to get what you're saying. Go on."

"Well, there are some clever people, in Japan, and elsewhere, working on brain patterns, and it turned out that we did know the right people after all. They devised a rig that doesn't show – goes under the hat that Nick always wears on stage, and feeds back to some stuff in the backline."

"The Feelers I heard someone talk about the other day?"

"Yep, them. The Feelers make sense of the crap coming from Nick. Then there's a whole load of computer shit goes on. Sorting out the useful stuff from the other stuff that Nick's thinking about – playing the solo, is he going to score with that groupie, whatever, okay?"

"Okay."

"Part of that was me," Pig said with a little pride. "Fluid mechanics teaches you a lot about non-linear equations. Don't look at me like that as if I was Einstein or someone. Jesus." He called for two more Bloody Marys. "So there we are, a few PhDs in the road crew later, and quite a lot of lines of computer program written. Then we had to interpret what we had just sorted out, and that took a bit of doing, I can tell you. What pattern represented what, and how we could sort out just what was going on in the audience."

"I wouldn't know where to start."

"We found out the best way was to take what we called cross-bearings. That's to say, we took another set of readings, and match them up against what we got from Nick."

"Bobby?"

"Give the man a coconut. Yep, Bobby. She wasn't too keen on the idea. By this time, though, we'd miniaturised the gizmo so that it looked like a pendant, and could fit the tickly bits at the back of her head under her hair. Once we had Bobby's data in there to compare with Nick's, it was pretty easy to find out what the useful bits were and make more sense of it all."

"And how did you work out how this all tied in with the audience's real reactions?"

"We put pollsters outside the gig, asking some questions. Posed as market research, which it was, but very crude compared with what Nick and Bobby were getting."

"What sort of things?"

"Oh, we could tell almost exactly what they were worried about, and what weight each worry should represent on a scale. Money, sex, drugs, politics, whatever. We even got so that we could predict to a decimal place what percentage would be prepared to go on an anti-whaling demo, for example, or how many would welcome a Bulgarian as a next-door neighbour."

"That's impossible. All Nick and Bobby are doing are picking up feelings."

Pig smiled. "It's real, believe me. All it takes is a whole lot of number-crunching, and that's what we do when we're not on the road. The road trips collect a shitload of data. We bring it back, and we stuff it into the machines back at the Permanent Hutch. We've got more blade servers there than a lot of big businesses. I'm not saying it's all been cheap, but we get our money back off it."

"And you're selling this to the ad agencies and the market research people? So that the poor proles can be suckered into buying more stuff they don't need and can't afford?"

"I knew Nick had you figured right," said Pig. "For a banker—"

"Ex-banker. Bastards let me go."

"OK, for an ex-banker, you're a raving lefty, aren't you? On the side of the little guy and all that."

"Guess being kicked onto the street does that to you, you know." Leo thought about it for a few seconds. "I suppose I've always had a bit of that in me, mind."

"Anyway, the answer to your question is no, we don't sell the data to those people. Bobby said the same as you – there's too much commercialism out there, she said, and she didn't want to be a part of it. She's got a heart, that one, just like you have."

"So you'd spent all this money and all this effort producing a whole load of highly accurate data that's no use to anyone."

"No way," said Pig. "That's what we thought at first, though. Crazy bitch has blown us all up, and we're up shit creek. We'd spent a lot of money on all of this, and we didn't want to feel it had all been pissed away on nothing. Then we found out – don't ask me how – there are some mad billionaires out there who want to change things the way you and Bobby – and me, if you want the truth – want them to be changed."

"You mean like George Soros? Bill Gates? That sort

of person?"

"Not Soros himself. He's too public. And not Gates, either. The people I'm talking about are people you've probably never heard of. They keep themselves to themselves, and they typically don't appear in the papers. Now I'm not the person who usually deals with them, so I can't tell you that much about them. But what they can do is to use the data we provide, and they can use that to determine the points at which they can apply pressure to make change happen. Sort of like that jujitsu thing. You don't need a lot of strength – you just apply it at the right point."

"And what you are doing is worth a lot of money to them?"

"More than you'd imagine. These guys are actually getting results."

"Seems to me that things are getting progressively worse. Just look at the state of the world now."

"I tell you, we – by which I mean the world as a whole – would be deeper in the shit if we hadn't been able to get the mood of the population over to these people. These are the guys who advise the politicians, and tell them what to do. They own newspapers and tell them what to print. I don't like to boast, but I'm pretty sure we've been able to bring about some really great changes in laws in lots of countries, and maybe done even more, simply by us being able to tell these guys what the average Killer Rabbits fan is thinking, and applying that to the general population at large."

"So that's what it's all about?"

"That's what it's all about," agreed Pig. "Mind you, I've given you the simplified kids' version of what we do. There's a lot of computing, electronics, number-crunching, and some serious brainpower behind all this. You in? Well, you're in as Bobby's roadie and whatever else she wants you for, anyway."

Leo could feel his face going red.

"Oh, you're there already? Congratulations. Make sure you don't hurt her, whatever you end up thinking or doing, or I will hurt you. Very badly. I've watched Bobby grow up from a kid, and I love that girl like a sister."

"I'll bear that in mind. Thanks for the warning."

"There won't be any more warnings, so make sure you do keep it in mind."

Leo thought a bit. "OK, so I have some computer skills, I speak some Japanese. But I'm not one of your wonder boys at this sort of thing, you know."

"Ah yes, there's more. There always is, isn't there? And this is where we need you, and this is why I am telling you all on your own without anyone to listen. Another two Bloody Marys, please," as the attendant passed. "Not all the other Rabbits knows this, but we're being ripped off somehow. It's all happening from Japan, and we need someone like you to help."

"How do you mean, someone like me?"

Pig held up his hand and started counting off points on his fingers. "First, I mean someone who speaks Japanese, and can understand how Japanese people think, but isn't Japanese. That's important. Next, we want someone who knows something about how banks and money work. Not everyone does, and the fact that you've worked in a bank is great. And lastly, we need someone who's lucky."

Leo was shocked. "Me, lucky? Look at me. Lucky? You're joking, mate."

Pig heard him out, and then shook his head. "Look at it this way. You stole three million pounds of other people's money some time ago, and you're still walking around free. That's luck. You walk out on your wife, find your bit on the side with her bit on the side, and walk straight into Nick, and a job with the Rabbits. You missed getting killed by one of Lurch's spotlights, Chaz tells me. A matter of inches. And now, if I read you right, you've got something going with Bobby, and I can tell you, man, you've struck it lucky there. She is a sweet kid, and you're not the first one there – you don't need me to tell you that – but you're the fastest I've ever seen her take to anyone. That's a good sign. No, you're lucky, even though it may not seem like it at times."

"You're an engineer or a scientist or something. How can you believe in luck?"

Pig shrugged. "Are you going to drink that last Bloody Mary? No? Then I'll have it. Thanks. How do I believe in luck? you ask me. Good question. The same way as I believe in Nick's and Bobby's ESP or telepathy or empathy or whatever label you're going to stick on it. It happens. We tried to measure what was going on – all the standard things you can think of, and a lot you probably can't imagine. We managed to really piss off Nick and Bobby while we were doing it – no-one likes to be thought of as a lab rat – but we came up with nothing. And as I hope you have realised by now, we have some seriously bright folks in the Rabbits."

"But it works?"

"It works a treat. And there's none of us any the wiser how it happens."

"And you say luck is the same sort of thing? Something that happens, but you can't say how it happens?"

"Right. You've probably found out a bit about the past of some of the Rabbits, right?"

"Some of them. Chaz, Duck, Scuzz."

"It's not just some. We've all got something we could go to gaol for. Me included. And none of us, as far as I know, is even suspected of what we did. Mind you, we play it safe. That's why we have all the silly names we use in the Rabbits, and the different passports and the rest of the crap. It's why we try to avoid booking in at hotels, at least in Britain. The band's fine, of course. They're celebs, with all that crap that's involved, and they use their names. But the rest of the Rabbits? We may be lucky, but no point in pushing your luck."

"But luck's more than just not being caught out at something you did, right?"

"Sure. Let me ask you something? You gamble?"

"Not really. Went to a casino in Portugal once. Sometimes put a few coins into a one-armed bandit at a pub or whatever."

"And you won, right?"

"Well, yes. Roulette isn't exactly a game of skill, but I came away with more money than I put in there. And I do seem to hit the jackpot on the machines sometimes. You're saying I'm lucky, then? And all the Rabbits are like that?"

"I tell you, when we play Vegas, I have to tell the Rabbits to split up if they want to hit the casinos. Too many Rabbits in one place, and the house starts to lose big-time. And then the heavies come along and move us out fast. They can't prove anything, because there's nothing to prove, but they know something is going on, and it scares the shit out of them."

"So I'm a lucky Rabbit?"

"A lucky Rabbit with Japanese and banking chops. Yeah." Pig drained the last of the Bloody Mary and crunched the ice between his teeth. "So that's the story. Tell you some more in a bit." He pressed the button to recline the seat, and in what seemed like only a few minutes, was snoring surprisingly softly.

Leo listened to him for a while, and decided to watch a movie which had recently been praised in all the papers. He watched it for twenty minutes, and decided that the critics had their heads up their arses, and changed to the music channels, where the first thing he heard was a song by the Killer Rabbits. Now he knew them a bit better, he could hear the way in which Nick's and Bobby's guitars played off against each other, and how they merged and complemented the other's lines.

Hearing her play naturally made him think of Bobby herself, and… It was time to turn off the reading light, recline the seat and tuck himself in under the airline blanket.

He was woken by an attendant offering him a hot towel and some orange juice. Pig was already sitting up, drinking what looked like yet another Bloody Mary.

"No vodka in this one," Pig said. "Still get the benefits of the vitamins, though."

As the attendants served them a surprisingly competent imitation of a traditional English breakfast, Pig leaned over to Leo. "We've got an interpreter already booked for all our business meetings. We've used her before on the last couple of Japanese tours, but I don't trust her as far as I can throw her. I reckon she's the one who's sold us out, or at least working for the guys who are doing it. I want you to keep an eye on her, or rather an ear. Listen to what she says to people in meetings and make sure she's saying the right sort of thing. Listen to the phone calls she makes when she's meant to be representing our interests. My guess is that the little shit is looking after someone else's interests, but we've had no way to check it."

"Right. My Japanese is okay, but it's rusty. You'll have to give me a couple of days to get back into the swing of things."

"No worries."

"And what else is there to worry about?"

"That depends on what you find out from Ms. Reiko Nakamura and her conversation. It may be that I am barking up the wrong tree altogether, but I don't think I am."

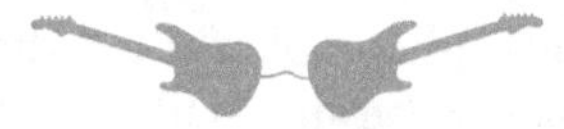

Chapter 10

As the Rabbits left the Customs hall at Narita, they were met by the tour organisers' representatives, including the infamous Reiko Nakamura.

Leo wasn't sure what sort of person he was expecting, but he wasn't prepared for a glamorously dressed young woman in a short skirt and skimpy top that left little to the imagination. As Pig had suggested to him as they left the plane, he made a point of sitting next to her on the hired bus that was to be the Rabbits' transport in Japan.

"Is this your first time in Japan?" she asked him in almost unaccented American English as she handed him her business card.

"No, I've been here before a couple of times."

"So you speak Japanese?"

"No, no," he protested. "I learned to say 'please' and 'thank you' and that was about it. I'm afraid we're going to have to rely on you for all our business."

"That's fine. You can trust me," she said.

Now that he was looking at her closer, Leo could see that Reiko ("please call me Reiko. Nakamura-san sounds much too formal.") was older than her dress and make-up made her out to be. There were crows'-feet around her eyes, and looking at her knuckles (which he had always found to be a fairly reliable guide to age), Leo guessed her to be in her mid-forties. It was always difficult to judge the age of Asian women, he found, but they were often much older than you expected.

Her skirt, which had seemed absurdly short when she was standing, now seemed even shorter as it rode up her leg. Despite himself, Leo couldn't help looking, and Reiko obviously noticed the direction of his gaze, pulling her skirt down, though ineffectually, and placing her handbag firmly over herself. Somehow, Leo didn't think all of this had been accidental.

She seemed compelled to make small talk as the bus took them to the hotel, asking what Leo had previously found to be the standard questions that Japanese ask visitors, including "can you eat raw fish?" and "can you useFthe new foreign-owned luxury brands which were rapidly monopolising the high end of the Tokyo hotel business, as the Japanese hotels seemed to be about ten years behind the times. It wasn't what Leo would have selected, if the choice had been up to him, but Pig had explained that the Rabbits could easily afford to stay there, given that the bill would go to the tour promotion company.

"Which is a totally owned subsidiary of a Luxembourg company, which in its turn is an affiliate of a corporation registered in the Cayman Islands, which operates out of an office in the Bahamas," Pig had explained.

"Sounds complicated."

"It's meant to be. One of these decades the taxman will catch up with it, but by that time we'll be dead, or at least retired, and they'll have to extradite me from

Costa Rica or somewhere."

"Costa Rica?"

"Yeah. Good healthcare system, great climate, cheap place to live, nice people, mostly. Can you think of a better place to retire? Which I intend doing well before I'm fifty years old, if you want to know."

Happily, the promoters had given the hotel the names and addresses of all the Rabbits (at least the names that were on the passports they were using) in advance, and the rooms were all assigned. The band got two suites. Nick and Bobby had one, and Leo and Kevin, the bassist, shared another.

Most of the Rabbits had to share twin rooms, but Leo had obviously acquired some status fast, and found his room to be a large single. Reiko had the next room, and she had made a great thing of telling him that if he wanted her "for anything at all", she was available.

Despite having slept on the plane, the jet-lag was already beginning to affect him, so he kicked off his shoes and lay on the bed. He had only just closed his eyes when the phone rang. It was Bobby.

"Come and talk," she commanded. It wasn't an invitation.

Leo guessed that she'd exhausted Nick as a conversational partner. If, of course, it was conversation that she was wanting. He had hopes.

Putting on his shoes again, he made his way to Bobby's suite and knocked on the door. Nick opened it.

Bobby was sitting on a sofa, looking out over Tokyo.

"Can you see Mount Fuji from here?" she asked, without turning her head.

"It's to the left from here," said Leo, taking his bearings. "Usually you can only see it on a clear day after it's been raining, or something like that."

"It's an ugly city, isn't it?" she said, after a pause. "It looks pretty at night with all the lights and everything. And then the sun comes up, and all it is is grey boxes."

"Have a seat," Nick said to Leo, waving him towards a chair. "Drink? How many Bloody Marys did you and Pig get through?"

"Pig and his bloody Bloody Marys," said Bobby. "One flight to New York he helped me get through eight of the things. Couldn't stand the sight of tomato juice for six months afterwards."

"Gin and tonic, please," said Leo. "I'll get it. Just show me where things are."

"Don't worry," Nick said. "Bobby?"

"Gin and tonic sounds good to me. Let's play the mad dogs and Englishmen game."

Leo had never had a drink prepared for him by a rock star before. Didn't taste much different from the usual gin and tonic, though. Bobby accepted hers, and turned round to face Leo as Nick moved to sit beside her on the sofa.

"So Pig has told you all about us, then?" Nick said. "Cheers." They all raised their glasses. "And what we do and how we go about doing it?"

"Right."

"You have a problem with any of this?" asked Bobby. "Because it doesn't matter what Pig may have said to you. There is a way out for you if you want there to be."

"No," Leo said. He looked from Nick to Bobby and back again. There was a family resemblance, but it was more in their attitudes and they way that they held themselves than it was in their faces. "I'm good with it."

"You've got three million quid in a bank here," said

Nick. "Tell me honestly, do you think you can get hold of it?"

"I'm pretty sure I can."

"In cash?"

"I suppose so, but there are all sorts of regulations about money laundering and so on. But yeah, Japan's a very cash-based society. Why?"

"We – that is to say, the Rabbits – might need some cash pretty soon. Large amounts of it, here in Japan."

"Has to be cash, right?"

"Yep. The kind of people we might end up talking to won't take credit cards." Bobby smiled at him.

"This isn't necessarily going to be on the right side of the law?"

"What's the 'right' side, when the laws themselves are wrong?" Nick asked.

"Point."

"And how much of this three million do you need?"

"Most of it, probably."

"Will you pay me back? With interest?"

Nick laughed. "There speaks an ex-banker. Maybe, if you insist."

"It's a lot of money to be giving away."

"We're in the position where we could lose a lot of money," said Bobby. "And we need to stop it before it happens."

"What's happening?" asked Leo.

"Pig's told you about the Feelers, and how they get all the information from Bobby and me, right? Well, that isn't really data until it's been sliced and diced, so we have no idea what's good and what's bad till we get back home and run it all through that computer system there."

"Up until about a year ago, everything was fine."

Bobby picked up the story. "And then things started to go really crazy. When the data had all been analysed, it made no sense."

"How so?"

"Well, just suppose we played three nights in Nottingham," said Nick.

"Actually, this isn't a 'suppose' – this is what actually happened," said Bobby.

"All right. We played three gigs in Nottingham on three successive nights. And we were being asked by one of our clients – he owns a big interest in several newspapers in Belgium and France – about people's attitudes to European military intervention in the Middle East. Believe it or not, that's the sort of thing we've been able to give pretty definite figures on. So when we get back, that's what we're trying to tease out of the three nights' data."

"First night," said Bobby, "we get this peace and love and hippy result that over eighty percent of the audience love Muslims, have no problem with Arab countries, would let their sister marry a Muslim, would convert to Islam themselves, whatever, whatever. Everything in the garden's lovely, right?"

"And the next night," said Nick, tag-teaming her, "same venue, same sort of audience, same everything, except it's a different night, the results show the complete opposite. Over eighty percent of the audience wants European armies to march into the Middle East, set fire to the whole lot, nuke it for good measure, and piss all over what's left. Same sort of audience, basically. Nothing in the news or anything to change their minds. We checked."

"And the last night – it's a fifty-fifty split, pro-Muslim supporters, anti-Muslim bigots. Which we don't think is the right answer, by the way. Basically, we were left with a heap of steaming crap. There is no way we could go back to our Belgian friend and ask him to pay up. There really wasn't any sort of data we could make sense out of. So riddle me this, why do we get three different answers on three different nights?"

"Equipment failure?" suggested Leo.

"That's a pretty weird failure, wouldn't you say? And the night after that we played Reading, and all the results were what we would expect. With the same gear. No changes, no swap-outs."

"Someone playing around with the raw data?"

"Who? Those Feelers which record the data are pretty secure. The data's all encrypted, it's time-stamped. It would have to be an inside job. Not that we didn't consider that. But there's only two or three people who would be able to reconstruct the avocado from the guacamole, if you get my meaning, and Bobby and I know for sure that it's not them."

"How do you know for sure? Oh," as he realised. "Your empathy or whatever?"

"Yep. We can tell if someone's not telling the truth."

"Must be useful."

"It is," Nick said simply. "Of course, we can't tell if someone is sincerely deluding themselves. That's a different matter. But that's not something where you could lie convincingly to yourself, is it?"

"OK, so the raw data is out of court as a culprit. How about the guacamole, as you describe it? Could someone have had a go at that at some point?"

"Yes, of course they could, but again, we are positive it's not in the Rabbits."

"Some sort of weird software bug in the analysis stage? We had one in the bank once, which did strange things if a customer's balance was in credit by less than a pound when midnight rolled around. Credited them with another hundred pounds. Just a bug in the programmer's logic. Forgot to move a decimal point or something."

"It's another thing we thought of. We did go through the code – well, not Nick and me, but the Rabbits who are good at that sort of thing – and there was nothing. But you're thinking along the same lines as us, which is good."

"I take it this isn't the only time this has happened?"

"It's not a regular thing," said Nick, "but it's happened often enough recently that we really can't trust ourselves any more. And the real bugger of the thing is that we don't know until after we get back and start crunching numbers."

"Why don't you send the data back over the Internet before you return? Does it all have to live in the system till then?"

"It's a lot of data. Gigabytes each night. Too much to send back when we're on the road."

"Then use removable hard disks, and FedEx them back each night?"

"Might work. Talk to Pig about it. Good thought," said Nick. As he said that, Leo felt a sort of tingle in his mind which seemed to come from Bobby. A tingle of pleasure and congratulation. Silly to think like that, he thought to himself.

"No, that's not silly," Bobby said to him. "Nick, we've got another one besides us in the Rabbits now, you know."

"Thought I'd found another one when I met him on the street a few days ago," Nick said to her.

"Another one?" said Leo.

"Yep. Another one who can read emotions. Empathy. Whatever. I told you, Leo, didn't I, that I thought you might have that sort of gift?"

"Hey! All I got was a little sort of twitch from you," protested Leo.

"And that's more than many people ever get," said Bobby. "Anyway, if we can develop this talent of yours, it's going to be incredibly useful. Because we've come to the conclusion – that's Nick and Pig and Chaz and me – that there's someone coming to the gigs once in a while who knows as much or more about this shit than we do, and he's turning up the volume, or whatever, simply to embarrass us, and put us out of business."

"Why?"

"Presumably he's working for the other side. The side we're trying to stop. The side which wants wars, and inequality, and hunger, and all the rest of the crap that decent people hate. Your former employers at the bank, for example."

"They weren't that bad, really, I suppose. At least, they weren't running death camps or anything, but I get what you're driving at. Anyway, if that's what you think is happening, can't you just find him and stop him? Or her, I suppose. And why does Japan come into this? How do I help?"

"Too many questions all at once," said Nick. "Let's take them one at a time, shall we? Why can't we just find him and stop him? Because Bobby and I can only read the audience when we're performing. Something about the music; the rhythm, the volume, whatever, seems to really act as an amplifier for their emotions and their thoughts. When we're backstage, or while the support band is on stage, we really can't pick up that much. So it's only while we're actually playing that we're useful."

"And it takes a bit of concentration to play like we do, you know." Bobby smiled. "So there's no way we can really find the guy. Or girl. Or whatever."

"Next," Nick went on. "Why Japan? Because that's where we think the funding is coming from. We've got Rabbits who are really good at tracing what we call 'goldseams' – the routes that money takes as it flows around the world. And we've worked out that there's a Japanese connection to all those clients whose research was buggered up in this way. There's no other common factor. All of the evidence points back here."

"And so I get called in to help? Well, thank you very much for the vote of confidence."

"But you are going to help, aren't you? I mean, you know something about money, you know something about Japan, and I am pretty sure that you can help with the empathy bit." Bobby smiled at him. "And you probably need us to get your money out of the Japanese bank."

"Well, I suppose so," he said. "How common is this ability that you and Nick have, anyway?"

"Not really common," she said. "Or put it this way, not many people have it, know they have it, and have trained themselves to use it. There's a couple of potential empaths in the Rabbits, but I don't think they're any more than potential. You, on the other hand…"

"Something stood out when I met you," said Nick. "You can laugh about it if you like, but it's true. And, as Pig might have mentioned, you meet another Rabbit criterion. You're lucky."

"I still find that hard to believe," said Leo.

"So you don't feel lucky?" said Bobby, pursing her lips in an exaggerated pout, and batting her eyelashes furiously in Leo's direction, parodying her femininity.

"Is that what you mean?"

"No, you know what I mean…" Leo felt himself turning red, and made no further effort to defend himself.

"I'll work on you for the empathy," said Bobby. "You'll enjoy it, believe me, and I think you're going to start feeling lucky." She smiled, in a way that Leo found impossible to interpret.

"And tomorrow, you are going to go to a meeting with Yamagami Communications. They own several magazines, and have large stakes in various newspapers and broadcasters."

"And they are customers for the information that the Rabbits provide?"

Nick answered. "They should have been, but we weren't able to provide them with the information, because it was all so scrambled that it made no sense."

"This was a few nights after the Nottingham gigs," added Bobby. "Same tour, different set of questions. This was something to do with gay marriage and people's tolerance of that sort of thing."

"Anyway," Nick went on, "your job is to sit there at the back with Pig and say nothing as I talk to Mr Yamagami himself through our interpreter, who, as Pig has probably told you, can't be trusted as far as you can throw her."

"So why use her this time?"

"Because we want to find out exactly what she has been up to in the past. And if she has done half of what we think she has, she'll be sorry she even thought about doing it," said Bobby. There was a set to her jaw and a look in her eye that Leo hadn't seen before. He made a mental note never to cross Bobby in a way to put that expression on her face. "Up to now, we've had no way of checking what she was saying. So just sit at the back and make mental notes. Pig's there to look menacing, and to ward off any trouble that might look as though it might rear its ugly head. Yours is to smile and look pleasant, and to say nothing."

"You're just numbers, for face, as far as she is concerned. I've been told that Japanese businessmen always bring a retinue of useless followers to meetings who introduce themselves at the beginning of the meeting, and sit there for a couple of hours like waxworks."

"That's exactly it," said Leo. "It's the old feudal thing. The lord and his loyal samurai retainers. I get the feeling with a lot of these guys that they'd be a lot happier if they were all still wearing swords."

"So, tomorrow, downstairs in the lobby at 10."

"What do I wear? Rabbits T-shirt?"

"Did Pig bring a suit and tie with him from your house? He did? Good. Wear that, then."

"And in the meantime," said Bobby, "it's time for your first lesson. We'll go to your room. Nick gets embarrassed by the noises his little sister makes at times."

"I do not," said Nick, but Bobby had already stood up, and was dragging Leo by the hand towards the door.

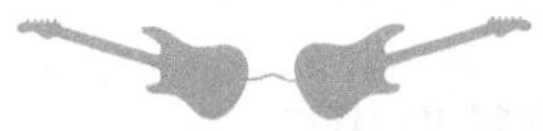

Chapter 11

Once inside Leo's room, Bobby took charge. "This isn't a domination session," she told him. "I'm not into that sort of thing. Was once, but haven't been for a long time. This is a training session, and I'm the trainer and you're the trainee, so you do what I say. Step out of line, and it's over. Understand?"

Leo nodded. He had only a vague idea of what was going on, and what was expected of him, but at least it didn't sound painful.

"Now you keep all your clothes on except your shoes, and you can take off your socks if you want. And you are not to remove any more until I tell you that you can. Understand?" she repeated.

Leo nodded again, as he bent to unfasten his shoes and remove them. He straightened up to see Bobby removing her T-shirt. She was wearing nothing underneath it today.

"Now, the way this works," she explained, facing him, "is that you have to sense from my mental reactions where I like being touched. We'll start above the waist, with my back. First, we're going to do the breathing thing again. Face me. Hands out, palms up." She took his hands, and they breathed together for about fifty breaths, Leo reckoned. "Nice, you're getting good at that," she said to him, and lay on the bed, face down, and called over her shoulder. "Just use one or two fingers to touch me somewhere, and listen with your mind for my reaction."

"This is really silly," said Leo. "Won't your body also react, and won't I be able to read your body with my fingers? What's the point of me listening with my mind, as you put it?"

"It's reinforcement," she said. "Try it and see. I think you'll find that the mental thing will come along with the physical. Close your eyes if you think it will help you concentrate. Whatever, don't look at my face. If you can synchronise your breathing with mine, it might help."

Feeling like an idiot, Leo watched her body and her breaths, and matched his with hers, before tracing a small line with his index finger at the base of her spine. Surely there were better things to be doing with a half-naked girl in a Tokyo hotel room, he thought to himself.

"There are," she said out loud, obviously having read his mind, "but we're not ready for them yet. Feel, don't think. Don't think, feel."

If he felt anything, it was that he felt like an idiot, but he dutifully tried to open his mind to her thoughts and emotions. There was a twinge of something, but he wasn't sure if it was his imagination or not.

"Try another place," she said.

This time he tried her upper arms, brushing each arm lightly with the tips of his fingers. Immediately, a sense of something quite different came to his mind, so suddenly and violently that he started and cried out. It was a feeling of unease and fear. He wasn't aware that she had flinched, or that her body had moved, but it certainly seemed to him that this was not just a fanciful impression on his part. "Sorry," he said, instinctively.

"Well done, you caught it straight away," she said to him. "That's really good."

"What? Why?" He was confused.

"Shush. I'll explain later. Try somewhere else."

He moved one hand to the curiously erotic dark sparse hair at the top of her spine, just below the nape of her neck. Immediately, she wriggled in apparent pleasure, and his mind felt her contentment.

"Sorry," she said. "I couldn't help moving just then and giving you a clue. Carry on stroking me there, and just listen to what my emotions are telling you."

This didn't seem so stupid after all. Maybe there was something to this telepathy or empathy business, or whatever it was. He really did seem to have picked up her moods somehow. He continued stroking her, and feeling her pleasure, almost as if it was his own.

"That's incredible," he said, after what seemed like hours, but was probably only a few minutes. "I really feel... I don't know."

"Well, I feel pretty good," she said. "OK, one last thing today. You probably know that for most people, including me, one boob is more sensitive than the other. Tell me which one." She rolled over onto her back. "And you're not going to see my face." She turned her head away from him. "No rough stuff with them, though. I'm quite attached to them, and don't like them being mishandled, even if they are only little."

They were small, he thought, but they were rather

nice to look at and feel. Dutifully, he tried to tune into her thoughts, as his hands skimmed her breasts, cupped them, and he ran his fingers round and over the nipples.

"The right one," he declared after five minutes' exploration.

"You had a fifty-fifty change of being right there, and you were indeed correct. Well done. Good students get rewards. Take off your clothes."

By the time he was naked, she had also stripped off all her clothes. "I'm going to fuck you," she announced, "like I did the other day, but with one difference. I want you to concentrate on what I am feeling, rather than on what your body's feeling. Lie back and enjoy the ride."

And with that, she straddled his body. Dutifully, he tried to experience her sensations, but found it impossible.

"You're trying too hard," she told him. "Lie still. Not just your body, but your mind should lie still and just relax and absorb what's happening around you."

It was hard to relax with her fingers and tongue playing around his body, but he forced his body to lie still and his mind to listen. Suddenly, in a wave, he made contact with her mind. She was listening to his body's pleasure and amplifying it, and he to hers and taking it and making it stronger, and she in turn was passing it back again to him, in an infinite spiral of sensation. The pleasure was beyond the threshold of ecstasy, almost past that of pain, and he cried out in a wild wordless shout at the same time that she did. It was impossible to say that one echoed the other – it happened at the same time.

And then suddenly it was over. She almost threw herself off him as if his body had become electrified as they came together in a white explosion inside his head.

They lay side by side, gasping for breath, not daring to touch the other. She was the first to speak.

"What the hell happened there?"

"I don't know," he answered. "Or rather, I do. You were listening to my feelings and I was listening to yours and—"

"Feedback," she said. "That was incredible."

"Never happened to you before?"

"Never done it like that before, right." She lay back, still breathing heavily. He watched her ribcage pulsing, her breasts rising and falling. "Do you smoke?" she asked him.

"Used to. Gave up a few years back."

"Me too. Damn. Could do with a cigarette now." She reached out a hand towards him, and he took it in his own hand. "You're pretty good," she told him.

"Not too bad yourself," he grinned.

"Well, that too, I guess. I meant about the empathy thing. You're getting into that, aren't you?"

He forced his mind to listen to hers. He could tell that she was being honest with him, and that there was something there in her liking for him that was more than physical attraction.

"Don't push it too hard, though," she said. "Sorry, I shouldn't answer your thoughts like that, but it seems that we're really synced up here. Never met it like this before. Not sure that I'm that comfortable with it yet, to be honest with you."

"What about you and Nick?"

"Well, obviously we don't..." She waved her hand to indicate the bed and their naked bodies. "But yes, we're in sync, of course. That's why we play the music together the way we do. I told you."

He made a sudden decision. "When I get the three

million out of the bank, it's all yours."

"You mean it's all the Rabbits' money?"

"No, yours. If you want to give it to the Rabbits, that's fine. If you want to keep it, that's fine."

"Sweet of you, dear," she said. "Let's not count your chickens before they're hatched, though."

"Time for a shower," he said. "You first?"

"Together," she said. "But no funny stuff."

"I don't think I could manage it again for a week."

"Want to bet?" She winked at him, leaned over, and kissed him. It was more than a friendly peck, but it lacked the mad passion of what they had just experienced.

A few minutes later, clean and dressed, she slipped out of his room, leaving him lying limp and exhausted on the bed, with a promise they would meet for dinner later. His head was spinning with what he had just experienced, but she was right that he was beginning to feel lucky. It certainly didn't seem like a week since he'd walked out on Gail to a Sharon who didn't want him.

And now he had to come to terms with something which was quite outside anything he had ever believed was possible. He was one of those telepaths or empaths or whatever they called themselves. At least with one person, under some rather special circumstances. He cast his mind back to the past, wondering if there were any occasions when he had had this kind of experience, but was unable to recall any.

He set his phone to wake him a little before he was meant to meet Bobby, and dozed off. He woke, splashed cold water over his face, and left the room, just as Reiko was coming out of her door. Coincidence? He hoped so.

"Going for dinner?" she asked him with a smile. Her skirt was a little longer than it had been on the bus, he noticed.

"I am going to meet Bobby downstairs and we're going for dinner together," he said.

"Oh. What are you going to eat? I know a really good sushi restaurant not too far from here if you want to eat sushi."

And if you come along too, Leo thought to himself. "Well, let's see what Bobby wants to do," he said to her.

They rode the lift together to the lobby. Bobby was waiting, androgynous behind dark glasses. She frowned when she saw Reiko.

It was impossible to see her eyes or her expression, but Leo picked up a question mark coming from her.

"Reiko said that she knows a good sushi restaurant near here, if you want to eat sushi."

Bobby said nothing, but just nodded. Reiko led the way to a place which Leo would simply have walked past, and sat them down at a table. She ordered three set meals for them, after first checking whether there was any fish or shellfish that they didn't want or felt they couldn't eat. Leo had never been a fussy eater, and Bobby simply shook her head when asked if there was anything she didn't want to eat. Though the place was rather dark, Bobby kept the aviator shades on, and didn't say a word throughout the whole evening.

The sushi, when it arrived, was delicious. Reiko was right, it was good – the best he had ever tasted, and it was too good to spoil with conversation. At the end of the meal, as they were sipping their green tea, Reiko got up. "I'll pay the bill and give you the receipt," she said.

Leo eavesdropped on her conversation with the restaurant owner. It seemed that the bill came to fifteen thousand yen each, but Reiko was asking for a receipt for sixty-five thousand.

She's ripping off the Rabbits, he thought to Bobby, but wasn't sure if the message was getting through. This way of communicating didn't seem to be too reliable.

Reiko came back brandishing the receipt. "I'll give it to you, and you can sort it out and repay me later," she said, handing the piece of paper to Leo.

As she turned away towards the door, Leo shot a look towards Bobby, who gave him an almost imperceptible nod in return. Leo tried to listen to her mind, but could pick up almost nothing.

«Never mind,» he heard Bobby say, so softly that he had trouble picking out the words. «It takes time.»

"You said that without moving your lips!" he burst out. And so she had. He'd been watching her face while she spoke to him, and he could have sworn that her mouth hadn't opened. Immediately he bit his tongue, worried that he'd given away a secret.

Reiko turned round, and his heart sank. "No, it's just that Japanese people don't move their mouths as much when they speak. I do move my mouth, look."

"Sorry," he said, recovering himself. "Silly of me not to notice."

Although Bobby's eyes were hidden by the dark glasses, he could have sworn that he saw her wink. Or rather, he felt her wink at him. This was going to be an interesting power to acquire.

On the walk back to the hotel, Reiko insisted on walking between him and Bobby, pointing out the sights of Tokyo as they went. "But you've seen all this before?" she said to him. "And so has Bobby."

"Ah, but it's different when you have a knowledgeable guide to point things out," said Leo.

At the hotel, Reiko hung about outside her room as Leo fumbled with the card key. Leo was sure that either she was looking for an excuse to invite herself into his room, or to get him into hers, and he was working out ways of how he was going to get out of this when Bobby walked up, took him firmly by the arm and marched him off to the suite she was sharing with Nick.

"You are not going with that one," she said firmly, when they were out of earshot.

"I was wondering how to escape," Leo protested.

"And there was a part of your mind that wasn't trying to escape."

He couldn't deny it.

"You're mine, you understand that. You go with anyone else and you're not mine any more. You're theirs. But then you're also ex-mine, with all that implies. Got it?"

"Got it," he replied. "Why the silent treatment all evening?"

"Because Bobby is a man, as far as she's concerned, and I'm not going to let her know otherwise. Anyway, she's fiddling the bill, you said?"

"I didn't say it, I thought it to you."

"Figure of speech. All right, it's not a lot of money tonight, but it makes me wonder what else she's been skimming off the top, and how many other little rackets she has going on. For example, I think she was responsible for booking these hotel rooms. At least her agency was."

Leo pulled out the business card that Reiko had given him earlier, and looked at it. "I don't recognise the name, but then I probably shouldn't expect to," he said. "I don't have a computer here, so I can't check."

"I do," said Nick, coming out of the bathroom. His hair was wet, and he was wearing nothing but a towel round his waist. "There's good WiFi here. Need to go on the Web?" He disappeared into one of the suite's bedrooms, and reappeared with a laptop. "Here you go."

Leo went to a Japanese Web search engine, and looked for the agency. The Web site looked innocuous enough, to be sure, but something seemed wrong. Suddenly, he let out a cry of triumph.

"Yes!" he shouted. "Either very arrogant or very stupid, or both."

"What?" said Nick, re-emerging from the bathroom, without the towel, and standing behind Leo, looking over his shoulder.

"For Christ's sake, Nick, put some bloody clothes on. I'm sure Leo doesn't want your balls tickling the back of his neck."

"Thank you, Bobby," Leo said. "I was wondering how to say that politely."

"No point being polite with Nick," Bobby snorted. "I learned that a long, long time ago."

"Well, thank you all," said Nick. He was now wearing a pair of jeans and the hotel's cotton robe over them. "What's up, then?"

"Look at this," said Leo, pointing to the picture of the Board of Directors on the computer screen. "Count fingers."

"Eh?" Bobby bent to examine the screen. "Three of them have their little fingers missing."

"Oh fuck," said Nick. "Yakuza."

"Yep, this is a yak company," said Leo. "Gangster-owned and controlled. Who did your due diligence on this one?"

"You'd have to ask Pig that one," said Bobby. "Nick, get Pig up here."

Nick turned to the phone, and punched in some

numbers. A few minutes later, Pig arrived.

"Leo here has already proved he's useful," said Nick in greeting. "Our fucking booking agency here in Japan is run by the Mob."

Pig said nothing, but raised his eyebrows as Bobby pointed to the picture of the missing fingers. "Yeah, I see," he said, running his fingers through his beard. "Not good, right? These guys screw up, they chop off a finger, eh, Froo?"

"That's right."

"So our agency's managed by a bunch of fucked-up gangsters?"

"Not necessarily that fucked up," Leo told him. "But yes, they did something in the past to make them say sorry the hard way."

"Leo's question was," said Nick, "who did the due diligence on these bastards?"

"We took their word for it," Pig replied.

"And in this case, who was 'they'?"

"Yamagami Communications."

"The same people who we couldn't deliver to. And the same people, by a weird coincidence, who are suing our arse for non-performance of contract," said Nick.

"And they're ripping us off, I'm sure," said Bobby. She explained about the bill at the sushi restaurant.

"Well, well, well," said Pig. "What floor is the bitch's room?"

"Seventh," said Leo. "Same as mine."

"Not really high enough," said Pig.

"How do you mean?" Leo asked.

"Fall from the seventh floor, you might bounce back. Some people do. Have to be at least the twelfth floor to be certain."

"There's a rooftop bar on the fifteenth," Nick added

helpfully. "Great views on a clear night. Take her up and show her Fuji or something."

"Are you going to… to kill her?" Leo asked.

Pig laughed. "She might wish I had by the time I'd finished. No, I won't hurt her, even," he said in answer to Leo's horrified look. "But by the time I've finished, she'll have wet herself, and I don't mean that in any pleasant way."

"Bitch," said Bobby, shortly.

"You did well," said Pig. "I was going to spend quite a lot of money on a private detective service."

"Let me guess," said Leo. "One recommended by our friends at Yamagami?"

"Yep," Pig admitted.

"And of course, they would either have found out nothing at all, or they'd have fingered a rival gang."

Pig nodded. "Looking to take my job, are you?"

"No way. You keep it. I'm happy where I am."

"OK." Pig stood up. "I'll take care of business. I'll see you in the morning."

"Don't worry. She won't get hurt, but she will be very badly frightened. Pig has his ways," Bobby reassured Leo after the door had closed behind Pig.

"So have these four-fingered agents of yours and their bosses," pointed out Leo. "They might see Reiko as expendable, or she might be the special friend of one of the bosses. Either way, you might want to consider leaving Japan permanently off the Rabbits' future tours."

"We wouldn't use the same agents again," said Nick.

"You wouldn't get any agents working for you here," said Leo. "Word would spread. Wouldn't matter if they were yak or not. The word would be out that the Rabbits are bad medicine."

"How the hell do you know so much about these

things, anyway?" said Nick.

"I told you I worked for a bank, right? I was in compliance, which basically means that everyone in the bank has to stick to the rules. A sort of internal policeman. And one of the rules in a bank is that you don't lend to the bad guys. So you have something called Know Your Customer. We – that is, the bank where I was working – made a loan to a property company here in Japan, and it turned out it was owned by the Sumiyoshi-kai, who are one of the biggest and baddest groups here. And Muggins here got sent over to Tokyo to try and sort things out."

"And did you?" said Bobby. She'd been fixing drinks – gin and tonics – and handed one to Leo. She perched on the arm of the chair beside him, and ran her fingers through his hair.

"They'd been smart about it," Leo confessed. "We had all the proof that they were lying through their teeth and that they owed the money, but they'd set up this really complicated corporate structure that made it all legal."

Nick was laughing to himself.

"What's so funny?" Bobby asked him.

"I was just thinking, here's Leo, meant to make sure that the bank keeps to the rules, and then he goes off and steals three million pounds himself. Gamekeeper turned poacher, our Leo is."

Leo squirmed in the chair. "I suppose so. But now the money's gone, even if I've changed my mind about it, what do you expect me to do with it? Give it to a home for lost cats, or something?"

"You've got to admit there's a nice irony to all of this, haven't you?"

"If you say so," said Leo.

"OK, you're offended. Sorry sorry sorry," said Nick. "Anyway, your story makes it more important than ever that you're at the meeting tomorrow. Should we count Yamagami's fingers when we see him tomorrow?"

"Waste of time. He'll be a front man. Nothing recorded against. The guys running him will stay in the background."

"Well, let's see what you can do."

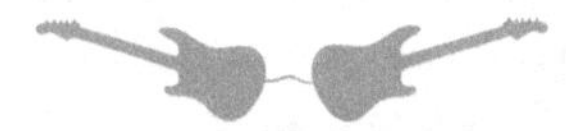

Chapter 12

They set off the next day for the Yamagami Communications office in a hired limousine: Nick, Leo, Pig, and Mr Ohara, an interpreter procured by the hotel. Reiko had been declared too ill to attend the meeting, and Pig explained that Lurch was "taking care of her". He didn't elaborate, and Leo didn't ask any more. Pig seemed to be in a good mood, whistling tunelessly and irritatingly until Nick begged him to stop.

At the offices, they were met by a fluttering young lady in a company uniform, who met them at the reception desk and made sure that they had security badges. Nick was dressed in a formal suit and tie, with his ponytail discreetly tucked out of sight. Leo was dressed in his banker's blue suit, with the Rabbits T-shirt, and Pig... well, Pig was dressed as Pig, and the girl's reaction to the greasy jeans and denim waistcoat over the Rabbits T-shirt showed in her face. Even so, she bowed them along the corridor to a room overlooking the Imperial Palace grounds, furnished with steel and leather chairs, which seemed to be about a foot off the ground. Leo sank into one, and nearly banged his chin on his knees.

Their guide said something to Ohara, who asked Nick and Pig and Leo what they would like to drink.

"Green tea, *o-cha*, please," said Leo. "And the same for them."

"Hate the stuff," said Pig. "Tastes like someone's emptied a lawnmower into a kettle."

"Good manners," said Leo. "Go with the flow and all that."

"All right, if you think it's a good idea."

The tea arrived, in small handleless cups with wooden saucers. Pig picked his up, and sniffed at it. "Do you actually like this stuff?" he asked curiously.

Ohara said nothing, but looked straight ahead during this conversation. He hadn't touched his tea.

Yamagami strode into the room, followed by two anonymous dudes, clone salarymen in suits and ties. Not Leo's idea of a typical Japanese executive, who typically tended to be on the far side of seventy, with expensive comb-overs of dyed hair, or with an immaculately coiffed mane of silver hair, and dressed in overpriced ill-fitting suits made from cheap fabric. Yamagami looked like a Japanese version of a young Steve Jobs, complete with jeans and black turtleneck. He presented business cards to them, but only Ohara from the Rabbits' party was able to return the compliment.

"I very much regret that my father is unable to join us today," he said in over-impeccable American English as they resettled themselves into the hammock-like chairs. "Unfortunately, he caught a slight cold yesterday, and he had no wish to pass on the infection to you."

Leo tried to pick up thoughts from the young man.

"I hope that he will get better soon," Nick answered.

"Oh, I am sure he will. It's just a slight chill, which he caught playing golf. He's taking it easy at home today."

Suddenly, Leo knew with certainty that Yamagami was lying. Not only that, he knew that the older Yamagami was in the next room, watching and listening to the meeting on closed-circuit TV, with the cameras hidden in the wall facing them. He tried to keep his face expressionless as Yamagami continued. "Now, Mr Lakone," he said, "we had a contract, did we not?"

Nick said nothing, but merely nodded.

"You were to supply us with statistics on public opinion on the subject of world peace, were you not, specifically on those topics outlined here." He snapped his fingers, and one of the aides passed him a piece of paper, which he skimmed across to Nick. "I am sure you recognise those points, Mr Lakone?"

"Of course," said Nick. Beside Leo, Pig cracked his knuckles. Yamagami looked across in his direction.

"Do you mind not doing that, Mr... Pig? It upsets me."

"Sure," said Pig affably. "No Mr needed, by the way. It's just Pig."

"Anyway, Mr Lakone, we seem to have a problem. The date for delivery was nearly four months ago. And there was a clause in the contract which related to late delivery, was there not?"

"There was," said Pig, bringing out some papers from somewhere inside the greasy waistcoat. "Clause 10, sub-section c, if I remember rightly." He licked the tip of one grimy finger and riffled through the papers. "Yes, 10.c."

Yamagami looked at him, as though one of the chairs had just spoken. "Excuse me, Mr er... Pig. But may I ask why you are involved?"

"I happen to be Mr Lakone's adviser in this matter," replied Pig. His voice had changed, Leo noticed, to an educated and smooth voice which bore little relation to the "biker" voice that Leo had come to associate with him.

"Are you a lawyer?"

"By avocation, yes, though not by qualification," replied Pig, almost urbanely. "I may well have seen and dealt with more contracts in the course of my short life, Mr Yamagami, than even you have in yours."

"Maybe you have," said Yamagami, "but the fact still remains that according to this contract, clause 10c, as you so rightly remembered, the Killer Rabbits organisation owes Yamagami the sum of approximately three and a half million dollars for non-performance."

"Well, if you pay us the three and a half million dollars that you owe us, we can call it quits, then, can't we?"

Yamagami stiffened in his chair. Leo was amused to see the two clones mimic their master and sit forward in their chairs. "Excuse me ... Pig. You are well-named, I will say." Don't do it, Pig, Leo thought at him, as he watched Pig's fists clench and slowly relax. "Or maybe you are just a comedian and you belong on TV. How can you claim that you are owed money by us, when it is you who have broken the contract?"

"Clause 12d," replied Pig.

"Clause 12d," repeated Yamagami, scanning the paper. "'Each Party shall use its best endeavours to aid and assist the other Party in the execution of the Services and in other business as duly agreed.' Well?"

"You were kind enough to provide us with a tour agency and interpreter, Ms. Reiko Nakamura," said Pig.

Yamagami frowned slightly. "That was my father's choice," he said. "Not mine."

"It is indeed your father's signature at the bottom of the contract," answered Pig. "As a representative of the company. I wasn't accusing you of anything. Not at this stage, anyway."

"Well?" Yamagami's attitude was stiff. He sat rigid, facing Pig, his hands on his knees. Leo picked up a feeling of fear, mixed with anger.

"Goodwell fucking Tour Agency and Ms. Reiko fucking Nakamura are a bunch of fucking thieves," smiled Pig pleasantly. "I do not consider that the recommendation of these fucking bastards complies with clause 12d." Pig's continued use of the four-letter word seemed to annoy Yamagami visibly with each repetition.

"Is there any proof that these people stole from you?"

"I had a long and intimate conversation with Ms Reiko Nakamura last night," said Pig, "in which she informed me of many fascinating things. You may find it interesting to know that she was initially reluctant to tell me these things. She is, however, recovering from the shock of having told the truth for once in her worthless life, and is resting at the hotel with one of our people taking care of her."

"Proof, I said. All you have is just words."

"Here," Pig said, and pulled out another sheaf of paper, which he tossed over to Yamagami. One of the aides moved forward, picked up the scattered sheets, squared them off, and passed them to his boss. Pig continued, "As you can see, it's a fairly detailed list of all the money that has been overcharged by Goodwell in the course of their services to the Killer Rabbits. I make it approximately two hundred and fifty thousand US dollars for the last tour alone. Either you were aware of the perfidious nature of these people, and you fucking bastards were deliberately negligent. Or, and of course

I would prefer to believe this, you are simply a load of fucking incompetent arseholes who can't be bothered to do proper background checks and due diligence. So, are you bastards or arseholes? Either way, you failed to use best endeavours, and the contract is therefore null and void."

Yamagami stood up, and ripped the papers that Pig had just presented to him into tiny shreds, which he threw towards the Rabbits' team sitting opposite him. "Now where's the evidence?" he screamed.

"You didn't think that was the only copy of those numbers, did you?" said Pig. "There's a copy with the Tokyo correspondent of all the major Western newspapers. If they don't get a phone call from me in a couple of hours, telling them that everything is fine, those figures, and the story that goes with them, will find their way into headlines round the world. And then you, my friend, and Yamagami Electronics and Yamagami Communications, are fucking history. Oh, and in case you are thinking of any funny stuff after that time is up, they are expecting messages from me every few hours to assure them that everything in Rabbit-land is fine and dandy. If those messages don't turn up in their in-boxes, or however I'm going to deliver them, then…" He drew the edge of one hand across his throat. "So are you still going to ask for that three and a half million dollars?"

"You'll never play in Japan again!" shouted Yamagami. "I'll make sure of that!"

"Save your breath," advised Nick, who had been watching the proceedings with an amused smile on his face. "We've already cancelled the Japanese tour, and we won't be coming back. We might even tell our fans why we aren't prepared to play in Japan."

"And by the way, no cancellation fees are payable," added Pig, "for the same reason that we don't owe you any money on this contract." In direct imitation of Yamagami, he stood up, and tore his copy of the contract into tiny shreds, before scattering it like confetti over the two aides.

Yamagami glared, but Pig's sheer physical presence acted as a deterrent while Nick and Leo left the room, followed by the interpreter, Ohara, who had sat in unneeded silence for the whole of the meeting, seemingly terrified out of his wits.

"Jesus fucking Christ!" Leo said to Pig when they were in the limousine. "That took balls to do all that. And a lot of hard work to get all that together."

Pig shrugged. "Poor little Ms. Nakamura," he smiled. "Actually, she's not that bad a person once she gets talking. Don't worry, she's coming back to the UK with us. I pointed out to her that she had a choice. She could say nothing to me, and I could leave her here in Japan, where her bosses would not believe that she'd kept quiet, and they'd make sure she never talked again. Or she could tell me what she knew, and we'd take her out of the country. She talked."

"And Scuzz is working on her new passport now?" Nick asked.

"Right."

"Good work, Pig. How much did we lose from these bastards over the years?"

"About a million and a half US. I upped it a little to Yamagami just now, but it worked, didn't it?"

Nick whistled. "The fucking slimy bastards."

"My thoughts exactly, boss," said Pig.

"Thanks for backing me up on the decision to quit the tour," Nick said to Pig. "I decided that when I heard that little bastard start to threaten us."

"You only decided in the meeting just now?" Leo asked him incredulously. "You didn't know what was going to happen? And you cancelled a three-week tour?"

"Yep," said Nick casually.

"It's going to cost a small fortune, even without the compensation to the concert organizers. All those cancelled plane tickets, getting new tickets, hotel cancellations, flying the gear home at short notice, all of it."

"Forget the gear," said Nick. "We'll leave it here."

"Except the Feelers," Pig pointed out.

"Except the Feelers. And the guitars, of course," Nick agreed.

"So the small fortune becomes an even bigger fortune," said Leo.

"We have a big fortune here in Japan," said Pig.

"You do?" Leo realised that Nick and Pig were looking at him in what could only be described as a meaningful way. "Oh, I see. But I'd told Bobby that I would let her have the money, and she would decide what to do with it."

"She'll agree with us, once we explain the situation to her," Nick assured him.

"Which bank is the money in?" Pig asked.

Leo told them. "But I'm going to have to go to the head office, and I really do need a shirt and tie for this. Sorry about the Rabbits T-shirt, but they're not going to take me seriously if I go in wearing that."

"Do you want Pig to go with you?"

"If I'm going to walk out with three million quid in cash, I'd sooner have someone Pig's size with me, yes."

"OK, we'll go back to the hotel, and you can change, and then it's off to the bank for you and Pig. How long will it take?"

"No idea. Could happen in half an hour, could take the rest of the day."

"OK. Just Pig to go with you?"

"A couple more people would be nice."

"You got it," said Pig. "Do you want us to wear ties?"

"No, just me."

"Thank God for that," said Pig. "Last time I wore a tie was... Do you know, I really can't remember the last time." He stared ahead, apparently gazing at the driver's rear-view mirror. "I don't want to worry you gentlemen, but it seems to me that we have a tail. A large black Mercedes with tinted windows seems very keen on knowing where we are going."

"Take the next right," said Leo to the driver in Japanese.

"But that's not the quickest way to the hotel," the driver protested.

"Just do it."

Obediently, at the lights, the driver turned right, just as the right filter was going off. Pig was watching the mirror. "Silly bugger," he remarked. "Light went red as he was going through it, and the police have pulled him over."

"For once," said Leo. "Police in Japan don't normally bother with that sort of thing."

"Anyway, we've lost them," said Nick.

"For now," Leo pointed out. "When we go to the bank, though, I'd be much happier if we didn't go out of the front door. Can you fix that, Pig?"

"I'll do my best."

Thirty minutes later, wearing a suit and tie, Leo, together with Pig, Chaz and Lurch, met in the hotel lobby. One of the hotel staff bustled up, and escorted them through the rear service entrance to a waiting limousine. Their move from the lobby was observed by a middle-aged Japanese man with permed hair, who spoke into a mobile phone as he watched them disappear into the bowels of the hotel.

Once at the bank, Leo presented his passport and demanded that all the money in the account be withdrawn and given to him in cash. Somewhat understandably, the assistant manager was reluctant to comply with the request immediately, and muttered something about money laundering requirements. Leo was just about to launch into a long argument, when the branch manager, a Mr Hirai, appeared from behind his desk. As it happened, this was the man with whom Leo had worked in the past, and he hailed Leo as an old friend.

After a brief conversation between Leo and his friend, there was no problem, and the money, in 10,000 yen notes, was counted, recounted, and piled into three lockable Halliburton aluminium cases which were presented to Leo's companions as "service" – Japanese English for something given away free to a customer.

With many bows and thanks, the four of them left the building and walked down the ramp to the underground car park. As they reached the point where they had left the car and driver, three burly men in dark suits approached them.

"You give us money," the tallest of them said to Leo, brandishing a wicked-looking knife near Leo's face. It was the first time that anyone had ever pulled a knife on Leo, and he froze. He tried to use the empathic skills he had acquired with Bobby, but his mind was too much in a state of shock for him to be able to use them. He was just about to tell the others to hand over the money, when Pig moved.

Bringing up the metal case he was carrying, he made as if to swing it at Leo's attacker's groin. The man instinctively moved both hands, including the one holding the knife, against the expected assault. Seemingly in the same motion, Pig raised the case to the level of the other's face, and smashed it against the man's nose with a sickening cracking sound. Blood spattered over the case and the ground, as the man screamed, and fell groaning to his knees, dropping the knife, which Pig kicked away into a drain.

The other two thugs had pulled out their own knives by this time, and were converging on Pig and Leo, ignoring the other two. As if it had been rehearsed, Chaz and Lurch moved their cases against the knees of the attackers, who howled with pain and shock, doubling over. Immediately, Pig leaped into action, swinging his case hard against the back of their necks, one after the other. The whole thing, from start to finish, had taken less than ten seconds.

"Time we were on our way," Pig said calmly. "Quick, before someone sees this rubbish and blames us for dropping litter." He half-ran, half-walked to the car, wrenched the door open, and flung his case inside before spinning round and watching for further attackers following them.

"Thank you," came a familiar voice from inside the car. Leo looked inside, to see the younger Yamagami sitting on the limo's back seat, a small pistol in his hand, pointing straight at Leo's face. The driver was sitting in the front seat, gagged, with his hands out of sight, presumably tied behind his back. "I believe there were two other cases, were there not?"

"Yes," Leo said. Pig had not moved, but stood as though frozen, his back to the car. "I suppose Hirai at the bank told you?"

"Of course. Hirai and my father are old friends. It wasn't hard to find out who you really are, especially as you signed for breakfast at the hotel with your real name this morning. Careless of you, Monsieur Gilles Fontaine," he said to Leo. He smiled, but there was little humour in the smile. "I take it my three were disposed of by your gorilla here?" He indicated Pig, waving the gun barrel a little. "Of course," answering his own question. "Well, there'll be time to settle scores later, of course. Maybe not now, maybe not this year or next. But some time, when you're least expecting it. But pleasure comes after business. So, the other two cases, please."

"Do it," Leo ordered, feeling sick. He'd been told by a friend who'd been trained by one of the companies delivering cash to banks that they were taught not to worry about the money, which could be insured, but about their own health and well-being, which were less replaceable. It seemed like a reasonable point of view to be adopting on this occasion. The other two cases made their way into the back of the car. Chaz and Lurch were obviously out of their depth.

"How are you going to get away?" Leo asked curiously. "Are you going to drive yourself?"

"Hell, no," said Yamagami. "He's going to drive me," indicating the gagged driver. "Once I release his hands, he'll be happy to drive me wherever I want."

"He's one of your people?" asked Leo.

"Oh no, but most people are happy to do what I ask when my gun is sticking in the back of their neck."

"And you'll leave us here?"

"Correct."

"Incorrect," rumbled Pig. He still hadn't moved from

his static pose.

"You said something?" taunted Yamagami. The gun moved slightly to point in Pig's direction.

"I said that you were incorrect. Or if you want to put it in simple English, plain fucking wrong."

"How so?" said Yamagami, leaning forward in his seat towards the driver. "After I unlock his handcuffs, all I have to do is—" He broke off with a gurgling scream. Leo looked with horror at what appeared to be a screwdriver handle, which had magically appeared in the side of Yamagami's neck, with a stream of blood flowing out from beneath it.

"You... you've killed him!" said Leo to Pig who was still standing immobile. His stance had changed, though, as his right hand was still in the position it had been when the screwdriver had left his hand.

"Hope so. Self-defence," said Pig briefly. "From what I hear of Japan, they don't look kindly upon ordinary citizens having guns."

"True," said Leo.

"So why don't you get the keys to the handcuffs, and let the driver have his hands back, and I'll dispose of the trash? If we move very fast, we may never hear any more about this."

Leo doubted this, but did as Pig told him. He felt a shiver of revulsion as he removed the keys from Yamagami's dead fingers – and he really was dead. Though Leo had come into contact with very few cadavers in the course of his life, he had seen enough to recognise the distinctive look of a body from which all life had fled. Also, though he hadn't been consciously aware of it, his empathic sense had been picking up something from Yamagami which was no longer there.

Thank God Yamagami had actually taken the keys

out of his pocket. Going through a dead man's pockets was an idea that revolted Leo even more than touching the corpse's fingers. He fitted the keys to the driver's handcuffs, and let the poor man rub his aching wrists.

"Tell him that he's not to tell anyone about this, right?" said Pig, who had dragged Yamagami out of the car, with Lurch's help. Chaz looked as though he was going to be sick.

"He asks how he's going to explain the bloodstains," said Leo.

"One of us had a nosebleed," answered Pig, who by now had stashed Yamagami's body in a dark corner. You had to look quite carefully to notice it.

"I don't know the Japanese for 'nosebleed'," complained Leo, but attempted to get the point across to the driver, who luckily seemed to understand. "He says he wants as little trouble with the police as possible, too," he said to Pig.

"Good. Nice to hear we're all singing from the same hymn sheet," said Pig. "Come on, all aboard the Skylark," he said to the rest of them. "Home, James," to the driver.

"How the hell did you come to learn to throw something like that?" Leo asked him. "And how did you come to have that on you?"

"A toolkit is a weapons kit, used right," Pig replied. "Isn't it fairly obvious that someone doing my job would always be carrying a set of screwdrivers around with him? And the noble art of defending yourself with a specially sharpened and weighted screwdriver is one that I have perfected over the years. Used to be able to get a treble 20 on the dartboard every time with it. Never had to use it in anger until today, though. Glad to know that the idea was a good one."

There really wasn't much of an answer you could make to that, and the journey back to the hotel took place in silence. Chaz still looked as though he was going to be sick at any moment, and Lurch, despite wearing an impassive mask, was obviously more than a little shaken by what had just taken place. Only Pig seemed to be unaffected by what had just taken place.

"Band members come first," he said, putting down the smartphone he had been tapping away on for the past few minutes. "Lurch, Chaz, as soon as we get to the hotel, book a limo to Haneda airport and get them on the 4:40 flight through Paris. Use the cash in one of those cases to pay for the tickets. You're booked business, they're booked first. Just done it online. Stick with them all the time – buy your way into the first-class VIP lounge if you have to – and make sure you are always in sight of someone in uniform. Never let them out of your sight until you're on the plane. Change the rest of the money into pounds and put it in the bank when you get back home. Spend what you have to in order to keep them safe. Chaz, give your case to Froo here. We're going to need what's in it." The limo pulled up in front of the hotel. "Chaz, get that limo booked. Lurch, get Nick and Bobby and the rest of them down to the front desk. We'll clear their rooms. No need to pack. Now, go, go, go!"

Chaz and Lurch leapt out of the car as the hotel flunky opened the door for them, and raced into the lobby.

"I'm impressed," said Leo to Pig, as they followed at a more sedate pace. "You got all of this done so fast."

"It was a plan B," said Pig. "It was all in my head already. Now the really hard work begins."

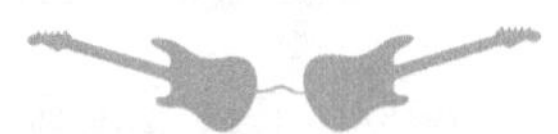

Chapter 13

What Pig meant by "hard work" turned out to be just that. He and Leo went to the suite which had just been vacated by Nick and Bobby, and used it as a command centre, Pig having given strict orders to the hotel that no-one other than a member of the Rabbits team who was already booked into the hotel as a guest was to be allowed onto that floor unless escorted by a member of the hotel's security staff. The hotel, used to such demands by celebrities, agreed to this.

Once there, Pig and Leo started to make online bookings for the other Rabbits. There was no way that they could find enough seats on a single plane for all of them at short notice, but somehow they managed to get bookings for everyone by the next day.

"And of course, we'll have to give them the cash," said Pig. "You're the banker. Call them in one at a time, and make sure that they each have enough to get to the airport, pay for the flight, buy whatever they need, and get themselves back to the Permanent Hutch once they arrive in England. And then make sure you and I can get home. "

It took some time, but that got done. While Leo was taking care of that side of the business, Pig was organising the other Rabbits, getting them to pack up all the musicians' belongings, and arranging for them to be shipped back to the UK. At last the suite was empty of Rabbits, and all of Nick's and Bobby's personal effects were packed up in suitcases.

"You're really going to leave all the backline amps and stuff here?" said Leo.

"Sure. There's nothing fancy about it. But the guitars and the Feelers go back with us."

"Where are these Feelers, then?"

"Right here in the suite with us. Nick always likes to keep them, and we set them up and take them down each night, even when we're playing the same place a number of nights in a row. They're right here, in fact." Pig pointed to a couple of flight cases.

"Mind if I have a look?"

"Sure." Pig laughed. "Nothing to see there."

Leo flipped the catches on the lid and opened the case. As Pig had said, nothing to see. A couple of USB ports, a few unlabelled LEDs, a power switch with an indicator, and a standard power cable. And a little plate on the back. Leo bent down to look at it. "Holy shit!" he said.

"What? Is it broken or something?"

"No. You didn't make these yourself, did you? I mean, the Rabbits didn't?"

"Nah. We worked out the basic idea, but got these made up for us, together with the headsets that Nick and Bobby wear on stage. They were made in Japan, as it happens. Why?"

"They weren't just made in Japan, Pig. They were made by Yamagami Electronics. There's a little plate that says so here. But I'm sure you knew that already."

Pig whistled. "That's what those Japanese characters

say, is it?”

“Not a coincidence, I think, between whoever made the Feelers and what happened today?”

“Too bloody right it’s not a coincidence, is it?” Pig paused in the middle of one of his endless stream of phone calls to what seemed like an impossibly wide range of contacts in Tokyo.

Leo put the lid back on the box. “You know, Nick’s been barking up the wrong tree, and so has Bobby.”

“Yeah?”

“Yep. They were thinking that there was someone thinking thoughts at them from the audience and buggering up the audience responses. Well, that wouldn’t work that well, really, would it? I mean, you’d just get sort of random results.”

“And they were getting results all one way one night and all the other way the next? Does seem unlikely, I agree.”

“But the weak link isn’t the link between the audience and Nick and Bobby. That’s just too much to accept, that there’s one person who can screw things up using this strange power to the extent that the results make no sense at all. And the computer software’s fine, you say, and I see that the link between the Feelers and the computers is a straight USB cable. Nothing fancy going on there.”

“So?”

“So if you’re going to attack the Rabbits, the weak link is between the Feelers, and Nick and Bobby and the crap they’re wearing on their heads. Right?”

“The data’s all encrypted,” objected Pig. He thought a moment. “But yes, if you built the system in the first place, you’d leave some sort of back door, wouldn’t you? Holy shit. You’re probably right.”

"And because the really clever bit of the whole Rabbit operation is the way that Nick and Bobby do their thing, that's what you were all concentrating on, right? That's the value-added bit. Everything else is pretty standard technology, and you'd tested it out to the max."

"Obvious, now you point it out and now we know who made this crap and what they think of us. Shit."

"Well, at least we know what to look for, don't we?" Leo pointed out.

"Yep. Someone with a high-powered radio transmitter in a particular frequency, using our encryption scheme. Well, it should be easy enough to work out some way to sniff out the bastard at a concert if you're right about that, and I think you are."

"The next question is why?"

"That's your job when we get home."

"You seem to be giving me a lot to do," Leo said. "And it's my three million quid that we're scattering about the landscape."

"Well, you seem to be good at it. You've come up lucky on everything so far. And there are those who might dispute whether that three million is really yours, anyway," Pig pointed out.

"Touché."

"You've booked us on a flight tomorrow?"

"Yep. British Airways."

"Business?"

"Of course. I think I can have a little say in how the money's spent, can't I?" Leo smiled. "Actually, it cost a lot more, but everyone's going business, including Ms. Nakamura. She's travelling with Letch. Scuzz has given her papers as Mrs Letch, or whatever name he's travelling under."

"He'll be into her knickers before they reach

Heathrow," Pig told him. "And that will piss off Cora and Dora."

"The two Rabbits he was hanging around before we left for Japan? They're not really called that, of course?"

Pig laughed. "Yep, them. Dora came first, and she was always poking her nose everywhere, so she became Dora the Explorer. She's one of the people who developed the software, by the way. Cora came later. She's a great drum tech. Knows how to get the best out of the drums and mic them up so that they always sound great. Got enough cash left to pay the hotel bill, after splashing out on all those air tickets, and paying for the freight for the other shit?"

"Easily," Leo answered him.

"Then everything's packed. We're carrying the Feelers, one case each. Pay if it's overweight. Guitars and all Nick's and Bobby's and the other guys' shit are going off in twenty minutes. I'll take care of that. Get your stuff packed up."

"Yours?"

"Did it before we set off with Nick this morning. I had a feeling there might be trouble."

"And you weren't that wrong, were you?"

"Nope. See you in the lobby in thirty and make sure you've paid for everything, including the limo to the airport that I'm going to order. Be there. We're off as soon as that's done."

It didn't take Leo long to pack, and he was ready for Pig, who had already ordered the hotel limousine for them. "Better than public transport," Pig explained. "If anyone's expecting us, they won't know where and when we're going to end up."

"And where are we going to end up?" Leo asked.

"We'll know when we get there," Pig said. They

loaded their gear into the back of the limo and set off for Narita, over 50 miles away.

"The driver's not the same one we had before," said Leo.

"I noticed," Pig answered him. "This one looks like an arrogant fucking prick to me," he added.

Leo noticed the driver's shoulders tense as Pig delivered his verdict on him. With no change in intonation, Pig repeated a variation in French. There was no reaction.

"I think we'd better be dropped off at the ANA Crowne Plaza Hotel at Narita where you booked us," said Pig.

"I never—" A sharp dig in the ribs cut him off short.

The ride proceeded in silence until they reached the hotel. The driver helped them unload their baggage, and then drove off to the other side of the hotel entrance. Leo could see him speaking into his mobile phone.

"And that's to tell the boys back home where we're staying," said Pig. "So we're not going to stay here." Waving away the hotel porter who offered to carry their bags, Pig waited until the limo had left, before motioning to the porter that their bags should be loaded onto the shuttle bus to the airport terminal.

Once on their way, Pig started to chuckle. "We have a choice," he said. "We can either stay the night in the VIP lounge, or we can pick a hotel at random."

"Hotel seems best. Which one?"

"The one whose shuttle bus leaves the terminal first."

They ended up at a modest but comfortable hotel where they booked a twin room. "It's not that I fancy you or anything," Pig explained, "but if the bad guys are going to find us, they'll have both of us to deal with."

"You really think they might?" said Leo.

Pig shrugged. "They might. And if they don't, there's always the chance the police will. We did leave a dead body behind us, remember. And whose money are we spending, again?"

"You've got me worried. I'm on edge now."

"Good. Stay that way. At least till we're back in England."

They caught the first shuttle bus of the morning from the hotel to the airport, and checked in as soon as the counter opened before making their way to the VIP lounge. "At least no-one's going to sneak up on us from behind," said Pig. "They've got to get through those dragons on the reception desk checking boarding passes."

Their flight was called, they settled themselves into their seats, and the plane took off. About thirty minutes into the flight, the senior flight attendant approached their seats.

"Excuse me, Mr Fontaine," he said to Leo. "And your friend Mr Nielsen," indicating Pig. "The captain would like to have a word with you, please. In the cockpit," he added, as Leo and Pig showed no sign of moving from their seats. They both stood up. "Please follow me," said the attendant, as he led the way to the first-class galley. "Please wait," and he patted them down. "Sorry about this, but we have to make sure that you are not carrying anything you're not meant to." Naturally, neither Pig nor Leo was carrying anything that could be classified as a weapon, having "cleaned" themselves before going through the security checks at the airport. "Thank you, gentlemen. This way, please."

The cockpit turned out to be surprisingly spacious, and instead of the masses of dials and gauges Leo had been expecting, there were several flat-screen monitors in front of the pilot and co-pilot. The captain turned round to face them.

"Thank you. I'm Captain Hammond, and I would appreciate it if you gentlemen could enlighten me on a few matters. I take it you both speak English?"

Leo was about to protest at this, and then remembered that he was travelling on a Belgian, and Pig on a Danish passport, and simply nodded.

"We've just received a radio message from the Japanese authorities," said Hammond. "They claim that two of our passengers – namely you two – are wanted in connection with a killing and assault that took place in Tokyo yesterday. They would like me to turn round and fly back and deliver you to the Japanese police. If I do that, it will inconvenience several hundred passengers, my crew, and last but not least, I will be extremely pissed off. It will play havoc with scheduling, and my bosses will be far from pleased at this disruption."

"Have they any legal right to demand this?" asked Pig.

"We are still legally in Japanese airspace," replied Hammond. "At least for the next few minutes. While we are in that position they have some jurisdiction over us." He glanced at the instruments, and punched some figures into a keyboard. "About four minutes, in fact. After that time, the matter is left to my discretion. I have a problem, gentlemen. I may have to do something that I have no wish to do. If, however, you can persuade me that there is nothing to all this, then I may choose to believe you."

"Would it help you make up your mind," Pig asked him, "if we were to delay talking to you about this for at least – four minutes, you said? For example, if I were to ask you what that particular control does?"

Hammond smiled faintly. "I'm glad you asked me about that. That controls the angle of the flaps, which reduce our stalling speed, and allow us to make safer take-offs and landings. It's very important that the flaps are always adjusted properly, according to the manual, otherwise we might come in too fast."

"And if that happened?" said Leo, joining in the game.

"We might run out of runway, worst case. Or come down too fast and too hard and blow a tyre or something along those lines. It's only happened to me once, but it wasn't a very pleasant experience, I can tell you."

"How long have you been flying, then?" asked Pig.

They kept the conversation going in this vein for some time until the co-pilot called over. "Out of Japanese airspace now, Colin."

"So," Hammond said, facing them again, "what is all this that the Japanese police are talking about?"

"Complete load of balls," said Pig. "Nothing to do with us."

"Well, since we're out of Japanese airspace when you told me that, I don't think there's any need for me to turn round. I think I will take your word on this, and I will simply radio Tokyo and tell them that there appear to be no grounds for suspicion. Thank you, gentlemen. Enjoy the rest of the flight."

And that, thought Leo, was that. Except that it wasn't. As he and Pig went through Heathrow immigration, they were pulled aside, and they were questioned politely, but very thoroughly, and questioned about the purpose of their trip to Japan. To Leo's relief, their baggage was not searched by Customs. He wondered how he would explain the best part of a million pounds in undeclared Japanese currency.

Their passports and papers came under scrutiny, but Scuzz had done his work well, it seemed. At any rate, their identities were not called into question.

"So what was all that about?" asked Leo.

"Probably the good Captain Hammond stirring shit," said Pig. "He's not going to be too popular with the Japanese authorities, and we caused a few problems for him, so he took it out on us by shopping us to the authorities here. Lucky for us that Scuzz is so good at paperwork, isn't it?" He grinned.

Leo hired a car in his own name to drive them to the Rabbits' headquarters, after discovering to his surprise that Pig didn't drive a car.

"Never have done," Pig said. "Never wanted to. Bikes, though, that's a different matter. Know anything about bikes?"

"Not a lot," admitted Leo.

"Had a Matchless 650 single," Pig said, seemingly oblivious of Leo's answer. "Lovely hunk of machinery. Fired once every other lamppost, and squirted oil over old ladies when it was stopped. Wonderful piece of Brit-shit, as opposed to the Jap-crap." He sat in the car's passenger seat, something as close to a beatific smile on his face that Leo had ever seen.

Once they'd arrived and unpacked, Pig set Leo to work. "Get on the Web and find out exactly why Yamagami might be wanting to pull this shit. You know your way round these things, don't you?"

With a groan, Leo sat down in front of a computer, and started to type away, finding his way through the pages of the Yamagami Web site. As he worked, he found himself being distracted by irrelevant thoughts straying into his mind, connected with Bobby. He found himself thinking about her and imagining what they had done in the past to an extent where he was unable to concentrate any further. He took his hands from the keyboard, folded them behinds his head, and leaned back, and then jerked forward with a start as he realised someone was standing behind him. He hadn't noticed anyone come into the room.

Startled out of his wits, he spun round, and found himself staring into Bobby's smiling face.

"Pleased to see me?" she asked him, grabbing his hands, and planting a kiss on his forehead.

"Of course," he smiled. "I was just thinking of you."

"I should bloody well hope you were," she said. "I've been standing behind you these last ten minutes or so trying to get you to notice me." She squinted at the screen. "What are you up to, anyway?"

Leo explained to her some of what had been going on.

"I always did get bad vibes off those guys," she said. "And Hideo Yamagami, the son, was really creepy. He knew about me somehow. Don't know how, because I'm sure no-one told him, but he was a real creep. Can't say I'm at all sorry he's gone."

"So you think there's someone inside the Rabbits tipping these guys off?" asked Leo.

She shook her head. "No way. Nick or I would know immediately if there was someone like that around. Believe me, we would know. And even if Nick or I didn't find out, Pig has his own ways, which are perfectly un-paranormal. Trust me on this one."

"Well, there's nothing that jumps out me so far. But sometimes, if you're looking for this kind of thing, you have to go through three or four degrees of connection."

"Will it take you long?" she asked. "Because I want you." She looked into his face and he was startled by what he read there.

"It's not just physical, is it?" asked Leo.

"No, it's not," she said. "And that's a fucking surprise, I can tell you. You're not my type at all. You're married, you played around while you were married, and I shouldn't be able to trust you a fucking inch, should I? You're a mess in so many ways. And I still want to get to know you better." She paused, and sniffed. "Love's a bitch, ain't it?" She dabbed at her eyes with the back of her hand.

Leo said nothing, but reached out with his mind to listen to what she was thinking. He was shocked to find a wave of sympathy and understanding, and yes, love, coming from her. "I don't know what to say," was all he could manage. "Yes, I like you a lot. I think you're a fantastic person in so many ways. But I can't use the L-word with you just yet. Give me time, please."

To his surprise, he felt a sense of relief come from her. "I'm glad you said that," she said. "And you mean it, too, I can tell. If you'd just agreed, I'd actually have been a bit worried. I'll be in my room waiting for you. Don't be long."

Just what he needed, Leo told himself. Some crazy woman who didn't really want to be seen as a woman hanging round his neck. The fact that he found her intensely desirable only made things worse, as far as he was concerned. He tried to put her out of his mind, and concentrate on finding out what made Yamagami Electronics, a subsidiary of Yamagami Communications, tick.

He'd had a little experience of untangling the ownership of companies in his time at the bank. It was obvious from the photos on the Web site that at least some of the directors were yakuza gangsters, but were they the actual owners?

He looked a little more carefully at what Yamagami listed as their product line on the Japanese side of their Web site, and discovered that most seemed to be custom products, made to order for customers, probably the Communications company. Well, that was presumably why they had been the ones who made the Feelers. So who were the customers? Not enough were named to justify what the balance sheet seemed to indicate.

So… where were the investors? He pulled up a listing of shareholders. The family, as he expected, were the major shareholders, and then a string of companies, which seemed to lead nowhere. Shell companies operated by the yakuza, he guessed, based on his previous experience. He noted with a little amusement, that the combined voting power of these together with the family was more than fifty per cent. The other shareholders were Japanese branches of multinationals, mainly American-based, and mainly the sort of company that the *Guardian* spent its time attacking.

Interesting, he thought, and printed off a few sheets of paper before going to find Bobby.

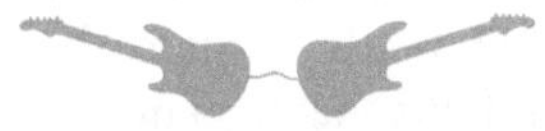

Chapter 14

Bobby was definitely interested in what he had to say as he explained how the Rabbits' Feelers had been manufactured by a gangster group with ties to arms dealers and other organisations of a similar nature.

"I guess some may be CIA fronts or something," she said.

"I'm not going to start looking for spooks under every bed," he said, "but you might be right there. It's interesting, though. The Japanese gangsters are typically linked to right-wing, or at least very conservative groups, but in Japan, that usually means very nationalistic, and quite often anti-American. They must have held their noses while they accepted that money."

"Or else the whole thing is a CIA front, and they simply hired the gangs to run it for them."

"That's going too far," said Leo. But it might just be correct, he thought on reflection.

Bobby was also thinking. "But why would Yamagami rip off the Rabbits in the way they did, if they could simply read the data going to the Feelers?"

"Greed," said Leo. "These people never have enough.

It's amazing, really. When I was with the bank we heard of one gang which was on its way to collecting most of a million pounds through some pretty sophisticated corporate fraud. They got caught for breaking open vending machines, would you believe, petty crime, and the fraud got uncovered then. If they'd stuck to big-time white-collar crime, then they'd have been fine."

"Like you did?" He winced at that. "Sorry. But you must admit that the money the Rabbits now have that you picked up in Tokyo – and thank you very much for that – is not legally yours, if we're going to be pedantic about these things. What worries me," she added, "is how much of the stuff that we've given out over the years has been a load of crap, and how much is genuine."

"You have repeat customers, right?" Leo asked. "Of course you do. That means that you were providing them with something that they wanted to buy again."

"Why didn't Yamagami or whoever it is doing all this just read what Nick and I were sending?" Bobby asked again. "And why would they try to rip us off like this, by telling us that we hadn't done our part of the contract?"

"If I understand what Pig told me, just reading the data that you and Nick pick up wouldn't be nearly enough. You'd need all the software and computing power that the Rabbits have here in order to be able to interpret it. And if what he said is true, you've got some really wacky geniuses here who are doing things that no-one else can touch."

"Guess there may be something in that," she admitted. "I suppose it's going to be easier for them just to balls-up our data than to try to intercept the real thing and try to make sense of it."

"The next thing is to see if there's any pattern to the ones which were messed up. The one that was done for Yamagami might have been just a way of trying to get money out of us."

"'Us'?" she laughed. "You're beginning to sound like a Rabbit, aren't you?"

"I think I've paid my dues." He was a little petulant. Damn it, he had helped the whole organisation get out of Japan. He'd handed them a get out of jail free card in the form of three million pounds. Stolen, at that. And he was probably an accessory to murder, or at least to assault and battery.

"All right, keep your hair on." She gently stroked his back. "Sorry to upset you. Yes, you've definitely paid your dues and then some. You're a Rabbit. No mistake."

"Tell me about the name," he asked her, leaning back, and putting his arm around her waist to pull her down beside him. She didn't resist. "Where does the name come from?"

"Well, it was one of Pig's jokes, really. We weren't always called that, you know. Before I joined the band on stage, the band was called something really macho and stupid. Not even sure that I can remember it now. I really hated that name."

"Wheels of Steel," said Leo, dredging the name from his memory.

"Yeah, that was it. I said I'd only join the band on stage if they changed the name. So as a joke, Pig said to the rest of them that I wanted the band to be called something like the Fluffy Rabbits."

"Wouldn't suit the music you play."

"Exactly. We have a bit more balls to us than that. And then there was all this business with the audience, and this idea that we could change the world. So I said to them, look, we're just a rock band, right? We're harmless really, but we've got this amazing power available which could end up kicking the whole world in the crotch. So we're killer, right? And then Pig said Killer Rabbits. Nick said yeah, I liked it, and the others – well, they didn't have much choice with Nick and Pig and me all for it. They thought it was a bit daft at first, but it fits."

Leo thought about it a bit. Yes, it did fit. "And then there's the bit in Monty Python. King Arthur and that lot."

"Believe it or not, that never occurred to any of us until later, when a journalist mentioned it in an interview. But by that time it was too late. We'd got the name, and we were sticking to it. So that's Killer Rabbits for you." She turned her face towards him and kissed him hard. "God, I was worried about you, you know. Chaz told us what you'd been up to. I had visions of you rotting away in a Japanese gaol for the rest of your life. I'm glad that's not going to happen." Her hand slid up under his T-shirt.

"Not half as glad as I am, I bet." He slid her T-shirt up and over her head. She wasn't wearing anything underneath it.

"Want to try that circular feedback thing again?" she said. "It was pretty mind-blowing last time."

"I still don't know what happened there," he said.

"Come on. Take off the rest of your clothes and stand up. We'll do the breathing thing again."

Leo felt that he was becoming an expert at this sort of thing, as he held her hands, closed his eyes, and synchronised his breathing with hers.

"That's great," she said after about fifty breaths.

"Now open your mind to me and I'll open my mind to you. And just do what comes naturally. We'll be guiding each other."

He put his arms around her and pulled her down onto the bed. This time she lay beneath him as they explored each other's bodies and felt the teasing sensations going back and forth between them. When he knew she was ready, he entered her with a gasp, as she raised her hips to meet him. It seemed that they were locked together for hours, teasing and coaxing each other to the brink, and then pulling back at the last minute. At the end, he couldn't hold back any more, and exploded into her, feeling her around him as she came, screaming a wordless note of pure animal feeling.

"Wow. Just wow," she said, panting. She was covered in sweat. "That was something else."

"It was, wasn't it?" He looked over at her. "You're beautiful, you know."

She laughed. "You're blind, darling. I'm a skinny ugly runt with a big nose and an appetite for sexy men, and a talent for playing blues-style slide guitar. And I can read emotions."

"What more could I ask for?" he laughed, and hugged her.

"I'm not going to answer that one right now," she laughed. "There are probably half a dozen things, but you're going to have to find those out in time." She paused, and looked at him with that special look. "You meant that, didn't you?"

"Yes."

"How about your wife?"

"Ex-wife," he corrected her.

"You're still married," she reminded him. "What about her?"

"I'd forgotten about her," he confessed. "You drive other things out of my mind, you know. When all this is over, do you think we could…?" He left the sentence hanging.

"When this is over?" she asked. "When is it ever over, do you think, whatever you mean by 'this'? And I won't even ask what you want. I know, and I can't give you any answer right now, can I?"

"Well, I meant—" he started, but was interrupted by a kiss.

"Never mind what you meant," she said to him. "You're very sweet, and I'm very flattered by all of this. Now it's my turn to say I'm not ready. Have patience."

"All right," with more than a hint of resignation.

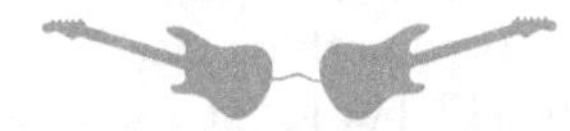

Chapter 15

It didn't take very long before Leo managed to establish a pattern. The "random buggeration" of the data, as Pig put it, seemed only to happen when the Rabbits' client was specifically asking for a question of peace or disarmament or similar topics. It didn't happen every time, though often enough to stand out among the other topics. Apart from the gay marriage question that Nick and Bobby had mentioned in Japan, this was the only subject where the data was so scrambled to be useless.

"So," Pig said to Nick, Bobby and Leo as they sat together, "we can suspect our Nipponese friends of making a deal with the Devil – that is to say, the arms merchants of the world – to screw these things up, so that we and the rest of the world have no idea of how people really think about these things."

"So we lay a trap for them," said Nick. "We persuade one of our clients to commission another survey and analysis on the Middle East, let's say Israel and Palestine, for example, and then we search the audience for whoever's screwing things up."

"Or we search through the Rabbits," said Leo. It was the first time that he had spoken in this meeting, and the others all turned to look at him.

"You're talking bollocks," said Nick. "We're like a family. No-one's going to do anything like that to hurt the others."

"We'd know if there was anything like that going on," said Bobby. "I told you that, remember."

Pig looked at Leo. "You're not just saying that about going through the Rabbits, are you?"

"Of course not. It must have occurred to you that someone knows what we are doing, and they also know the details of what we're up to – the clients, what the clients want, and so on. Who outside the Rabbits and the clients knows what we're up to?"

"You have a point there," said Pig, and stroked his beard.

"They could be hacking the computers," said Nick, but he sounded a little less than convinced by his own words.

"Sorry, Leo, but you're talking balls," said Bobby. "Look, Leo, I love you and all that—" She stopped, and seemed embarrassed, looking down at the floor.

"Go on," said Pig, gently. "Don't be ashamed of it. Happens to us all from time to time. Even to me."

Bobby looked up again and smiled, somewhat thinly, it seemed to Leo. "Even to you, Pig? I'll believe it when I see it. But Leo, think about it. Nick and me, we know these people. We've been with them, most of them, for years. Don't you think that we'd know if one of them was doing the dirty on us?"

"I suppose you would." Which actually left the people in the room as suspects, Leo thought gloomily. Which was impossible. "All right, Nick, someone's hacking the computers from the outside, then."

"So we'll get Chick onto it and bolt the system down tighter than a nun's pussy," said Pig.

"How would you know what that's like?" laughed Nick.

"That's for me to know and you to find out. Sorry, Bobby."

"I'm thinking," she said. "I suppose Leo could be right. I mean, whatever Nick and I are doing, we really don't know a lot about it, do we? I mean, we know it works, and we know that we can get some useful information out of it, if we put a lot of work in. But supposing someone knows more about this stuff than we do, and they can shield themselves from being read, somehow? It could be one of the Rabbits at that."

"We read all about this stuff in the magazines, and got every book there was on the subject, remember," said Nick, "when it was obvious that we had something going on. There's nothing been published about it anywhere."

"That's my point," said Bobby. "Of course nothing's been published. That's because it's all military secrets, and spy stuff and that. Look at what's been asked for when things go wrong. It's all war and security and that shit, right? You said yourself that this was all a deal with the Devil, Pig. The arms dealers. The military. The fucking Pentagon and whatever we bloody British call our Pentagon. Ministry of fucking Defence. Of course all this fucking shit is classified, and we wouldn't know a bloody thing about it."

"Well, that's a cheerful thought, I must say," said Nick. "One of our Rabbits is selling us out. I hope to God you're wrong there, Bobby."

"So do we all, I'm sure," said Pig, "but the way

you've put it makes sense. I wish it didn't. So we look for all the Rabbits who've joined us since we started the business?"

"That's only about half of them," said Nick, gloomily.

"And I don't want to sound prejudiced," said Pig, "but I think we have to start looking at the ones with foreign backgrounds before we go much further."

"Bullshit!" Bobby exploded. "That's just silly. If you're going to start looking at the Rabbits, then you look at them all, not just those who've joined recently, and certainly not those who weren't born here. Anyone could be selling us out."

"Don't agree there," said Pig. "Still, you're the bosses. Do it your way if you want, but I think you're wasting your time looking at every one of the Rabbits. Now, if you'll excuse me, I have things I must be doing." He heaved himself to his feet and walked out of the room.

"Where would we start?" said Nick. "I mean, if there really is someone who can put up some sort of shield against what we know, how the hell are we ever going to know about it?"

"Follow the money," said Leo quietly. "I'm good at that. It was my job, remember."

"How can you do that?" asked Nick. "How can you find out what's going on?"

"I have my ways," replied Leo. "Or rather, they're not really my ways. They're what all the thieves and con artists use to get into other people's lives. Social engineering, mainly."

"Meaning what, exactly?" asked Bobby.

"Basically meaning that I pretend to be someone else. Someone in authority who has a right to know the information that's being searched for. It's not that hard to do, and it's amazing how many people will fall for it."

"Can you tell us how it might work? Your social engineering thing, I mean?" asked Bobby.

"Want me to give away my trade secrets?" said Leo. "Okay, here's one example I'll give you for free. Most offices, at least most banks, anyway, you can only get in with a special card key, or you need to punch in some sort of access code. Keeps the bad guys out, right?"

"Right," said Nick.

"Except it doesn't, of course. Wear the right sort of clothes, and hang around the entrance looking lost. Say to the next person who comes along that you just nipped out for a piss or a cup of coffee, and you left your card on your desk. You're new here, and you haven't learned the tricks of the new office yet. They take pity on you, let you into the office, they turn left, you turn right, and you're in. Everyone just thinks you're new, and from another department."

"That doesn't get you into the computers, though," objected Bobby.

"Aha. Phase two. Find out where the help desk is, if you don't know already. Wait till there's no-one there. There's always going to be a few minutes when they're doing desk-side support or having lunch or something. Then you use their internal phone and say something like, 'Help desk here, we're having problems with the mail system. Can you just give us your password so we can check the mail queue?' The internal extension on their desk shows them that the call's coming from the help desk number, so it has to be legit, right? And then you're in like Flynn."

"Sounds far too simple. I can't believe that would ever work."

"Believe me, it works."

"Sounds scary," commented Bobby.

"It is scary. Really scary. People are trusting sometimes. You should see the sort of money that goes off to those African scammers. And they're not the sort of people you'd expect to be taken in by that sort of thing, either. Company directors, university professors, some of them. Greedy and stupid – it's a fatal combination, and there are too many people who are both."

"And you think you can get all the Rabbits' information that way?"

"Enough. Give me a couple of weeks."

It actually took him three weeks. During that time, the band was rehearsing songs for a new album, to be released later that year, and they were planning a short tour of smaller clubs and halls to perfect the new material. While Bobby was not rehearsing, and Leo was not working his nefarious brand of magic with the banks, they developed the mental links between them to the extent where they could, with a little effort, actually think words to each other almost at will. The sex they shared continued to blow Leo's mind – there was no other way he could describe it – and with it, the emotional bond between them grew stronger.

He almost believed he could settle down with Bobby into a quiet domestic existence, but when he tentatively tried to broach the subject, she headed him off at the pass.

"It's not me, sweetie," she said. "At least for a few years yet. I love playing the music, even if I don't like going on stage that much. And I can't let Nick and the others down like that. No, let's carry on the way we are for a bit longer and see what comes of it." His disappointment must have shown, either in his face, or in her mind, because she kissed him and went on. "Look, things are pretty magic right now, but it's early days yet for me. I'm just not ready to commit to anything at the moment. Don't sulk about it. Bless your peachy little heart, I'm not saying no for ever and ever. Just saying no for now, okay?"

He sighed.

"Listen, dear," she told him. "There's no point in building up your hopes over what might turn out to be nothing at all. And speaking of that, how are you getting on with your little tricks?"

"I think that I have an answer. But I don't like it at all."

"What do you mean? You mean you don't trust your methods, Sherlock?"

"That's the problem. Actually, I do trust my methods, and they're leading me to a conclusion that I didn't expect to reach, and I don't want to reach. But all the same, it's there, and it's not comfortable."

"You've only got a day or so left to finish. We start the tour on Thursday. You're the best guitar roadie I've ever had." She paused. "There's a double entendre there, isn't there? Anyway, you're my roadie for this tour, and I want your nose out of those computers and into my guitars."

"I know. I should have everything sorted out by then. Don't worry."

"And as well as being my roadie in the gigs, you've got to keep your mind open and listen. Not to me, and not to Nick, but to whoever's pulling this shit on us."

"Why do you think that something's going to happen?"

"Nick thinks it's going to. Some sort of deal he set up with one of the clients. He hasn't told anyone else the details, though. Just told me to tell you to keep alert and see if you can find who's messing things up."

"He doesn't trust me following the money?"

"He wants to be sure. Come on, it's time for rehearsal, and I want you there with me. Last practice, Chaz set up my pedals all wrong, and I want you to do it this time. You can leave your computer for now."

The rehearsal, which included the full lighting rehearsal, took place on a stage set up in one of the outbuildings of the Rabbits' base. The new songs sounded good to Leo's ears, but took a little getting used to. By the time they'd played through one of them three times, though, he was humming along with the chorus.

"I didn't like 'Light in my Heart' the much first time round," he told Bobby afterwards, "but by the time you'd finished with it today, I was singing along with it."

"Good. Because that's the one Nick and I want as the single off the album. One of my better ones, though I say it myself."

"You? I thought Nick wrote most of the Killer Rabbits' numbers?"

"Most, but not all. I do a few of them. This one's mine." She walked ahead of him, leading the way back to the dressing room. He felt her mind reaching out to him. «The song's about you, you know,» he heard in his mind, followed by the psychic equivalent of a giggle.

He played the lyrics back in his mind. «There's a light in my heart keeps on burning through the night, And what you do for me makes me feel all right. Though there's no reason why I should feel the way I do, There's something in that light that keeps me keep on loving you.»

"Yeah, corny, I know," she said out loud. "I don't

usually write love songs, but in your case, I made an exception."

"I'm touched," he said. And he was.

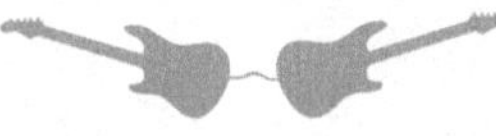

Chapter 16

The day for the tour came round. The Rabbit Hutch rolled out one evening, the Rabbits all aboard and sleeping through the night as the bus pulled along the motorway to the Midlands town where they were to play the first gig.

Because the venue was relatively small, the Rabbits were using their own PA system, rather than renting one locally, as they often did. "Better sound," said Pig. "We've got some of our own stuff in there to make up for bad sound at some of the venues. Designed by us, and you won't find it anywhere else."

"Let me guess. Yamagami made up the stuff, right?"

Pig narrowed his eyes and squinted at Leo. "Possibly. Yeah. Why?"

"Nothing. I just thought since the Feelers were made by them, you might have used them for other things."

"Makes sense, right? Nothing wrong with that, is there?" Pig sounded almost defensive.

"Of course not. Just curious, that's all."

Pig had been acting a little strangely over the past few days, Leo thought, but he put it down to pre-tour nerves, and the reaction to what had happened in Tokyo.

He settled Bobby in the room that served as her dressing-room, and worked with Chaz to get the guitars ready. He'd hardly spoken to Chaz since they had returned from Japan, and it was a relief to be discussing pedals and cables rather than money and investigating a possible renegade Rabbit.

As far as he knew, no-one except Bobby and Nick was really aware of what he was up to on the Internet. Possibly Pig, but unless Bobby or Nick had told him, he doubted it. Certainly Chaz seemed to have no idea what he'd been doing.

"Haven't seen you around for a few days. Bobby keeping you busy?" Chaz called across the stage to him.

"Yeah, well, this and that." Leo ignored the implications of the question, though it can hardly have been a secret among the Rabbits what had been going on between him and Bobby.

When everything was ready, Leo took himself back to Bobby's dressing-room. She seemed restless, and asked him the same question about her guitar setup several times, forgetting that he'd answered it before. Leo put it down to nerves before they played the new set in public for the first time.

«Do you want me to rub your shoulders?» he thought to her. «You seem stiff.»

«That would be great,» she thought back at him. «Just the shoulders, mind. No funny stuff before the gig.»

«Of course not,» he thought back, and started to massage her shoulders, feeling the tight muscles start to relax and go slack. He was amazed at how natural it now seemed for him and Bobby to be communicating without words.

"Yes, it's never happened like this before, I keep telling

you," she said out loud. "Sometimes I really don't know if we're using words or not. Tonight, though, keep your mind open for anyone who's going to start anything that might bugger up the Feelers."

"And if I do find anything, what am I meant to do? I've got to look after you and your guitars, right?"

"Pig will be standing by. Just tell him between numbers or something what's going on and he'll take care of things."

But as it happened, nothing happened. At least not that Leo could make out. Somehow he managed to keep his mind on the set, and hand Bobby her guitars at the right time, and change her broken strings, but there seemed to be no-one in the audience sending out hostile signals. No-one in the Rabbits, either, from what he could make out. The radio scanners that Pig had had put together to look for the mystery signals that had corrupted the data likewise failed to pick up anything that was remotely useful.

As Nick came off-stage after the encore ("Ladder" again), he looked at Leo and raised his eyebrows. Leo shook his head, and almost missed the guitar that Bobby tossed in his direction.

He packed up the equipment into the flight cases, and went back to Bobby's dressing room, to discover Nick sitting there with her.

"Nothing?" said Nick.

"Not a thing, either from the front of the house, or from the Rabbits," replied Leo. "Pig's just told me that the radio scanners didn't pick up anything, either."

"Maybe tomorrow night?" suggested Bobby.

"Maybe," said Nick. "How about the money trail?" he asked Leo. "Bobby said to me that you might have something going on there."

"I think I have," said Leo, "but I can't be sure about it. To be honest with you, I don't want to be sure about it."

"How do you mean?"

"I'm not going to say any more until I am really sure. I don't want to start casting stones until there's fire behind the smoke, if you get my muddled meaning."

"Whatever," said Nick. "Leo, you've done great. Not just all this business, but you're a good roadie. I knew it when I met you on the street that day. Anyway, it was a tough gig, with all those new songs. I'm pretty tired." He yawned on cue, as if to prove it. "I'm out of here for now. Look after Bobby, Leo."

"You're being most mysterious," Bobby said, when Nick had gone.

"With some reason," said Leo. "I really don't want to get into it right now, if you don't mind."

Bobby said nothing, but felt her ear, and then started searching for something on the table in front of her. "I could have sworn I had it when I came in," she said. "Shit."

"What?"

"It's an earring. I could have sworn I had both of them on when I came off-stage."

"What does it look like?"

"Look, here's its partner." She held out a golden hoop for his inspection. "Like this. Maybe I didn't have it here with me after all. Maybe it's still on stage or between here and the stage."

"I'll go and look for it. You stay here."

"No, I'll come with you. It will be easier with two of us looking. Anyway, I need some company, and I don't want to be left alone."

The old Victorian hall seemed slightly menacing to

Leo as they walked onto the stage. All the lights in the hall and on the stage were turned off, except the exit signs over the doors, and the only other light came from the street lights shining in through the windows at the top of the walls on each side.

"We'll never find the earring. It's too dark to see any-thing," Bobby complained. "I've no idea where the light switches are in this place."

Leo pulled out his small pocket torch, and was about to turn it on, when Bobby grabbed his arm. «There's someone else in here,» she thought to him.

«Where?» he thought back.

«Not sure yet. Can't see a bloody thing.»

Leo peered about him, and pointed. «More than one of them,» he thought. «Over there by the door.»

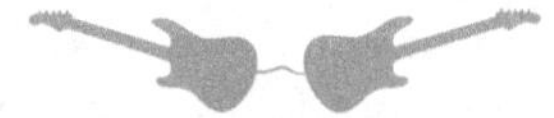

Chapter 17

Three men were coming towards the stage, walking fast in their direction.

"They're Japanese or Chinese or something," she whispered to Leo as she made out more detail in the half-light.

"I'll bet you they're yakuza," he told her. "Japanese gangsters, associated with Yamagami. Get behind me." He turned to face them. Better than being stabbed in the back. This wasn't something he wanted to get into, but it seemed he had little choice in the matter.

Now the three were close enough for him to see the knives in their hands. Wicked blades, and it looked as though they knew what they were doing with them.

"Run like hell," he told Bobby. "I'll hold them off." Like hell I will, he told himself. Even if he had been armed, there was no way that he could take on three trained thugs and hope to win. As it was… Behind him, he could hear the sound of Bobby's feet echoing on the stage, and then suddenly—

"Shit! One of my heels has just come off." Pain in her voice. "I think I've twisted my fucking ankle."

The first yakuza climbed the steps onto the stage, and approached Leo, who moved to block his path.

"I'm not a polite person," said the gangster in almost unaccented English. The other two stood behind him, unmoving. "If I was, I would ask you to let me past, please. As it is, I am simply going to tell you to fuck off out of my way."

"And if I don't?"

The other simply waved his knife in Leo's general direction. "I hope you get my point," he said, stabbing the blade towards Leo so that the tip touched his T-shirt, just below the breastbone. "I know it's a terrible pun, but most people seem to understand it fairly quickly."

"And if I don't?" Leo repeated.

"We're going past you to talk to her anyway, whatever you think."

"Are you going to kill her?" Leo asked. He hadn't heard her footsteps, and hoped that she had had the sense to move away quietly.

"Oh, no. We simply want to know where the big guy is. Perhaps you can tell us."

"The big guy?"

"You know him as Pig, I think."

"And why do you think I'm going to tell you? I'm not frightened of what you might do to me, you know." This was a lie. Actually, Leo was scared witless of what they might do with their knives. He had heard stories about the yakuza and their methods. Visions of parts of his body being carved off and held in front of his horrified face for his appreciation flashed before his eyes.

"How brave of you. But actually, we think that it will be easier for you to talk when we start work on your friend here." Almost before Leo could work out what was going on, the other two gangsters had slipped past him, and now returned with a struggling Bobby, one holding each arm, and with one clamping his free hand over her mouth. All she could manage were inarticulate faint squeals. Leo sensed her general terror, and her fear of what might happen to her.

"This one's a guitarist, isn't she?" said the yakuza.

"She?" said Leo, as innocently as he could manage.

"Don't fuck with us. The big guy told us all about this one. Let's see how well she plays with one of her fingers missing."

"You can't do that!" exclaimed Leo in horror.

"Can and will. Not the whole finger, you understand. Just a little reminder that it pays her friends to speak when they're spoken to." He seized Bobby's left hand, and stretched out the index finger. "I wish I could say that this isn't going to hurt you," he said pleasantly to her. "Of course, I suppose I could say that, but then I'd be lying. This is going to hurt you. Quite a lot." The edge of the blade moved to her finger, and there was a flash of steel in the faint light coming through the windows from the street outside. A strangled gasp and scream from Bobby and Leo's mind was flooded with her pain and shock. Leo forced himself to look. Blood streamed from Bobby's hand, and Leo felt he was going to be sick.

"No, it's just a cut right now. Nothing gone for keeps. But it could be a lot worse than that if you don't come up with a few answers soon and tell us where the big guy is."

"He's here," said a familiar voice from the shadows. Pig stepped out from behind a stack of amplifiers and confronted the tableau. He appeared to be carrying some sort of stick in his right hand.

"Well, well, if it isn't the man himself," said the lead

thug, turning away from Bobby. He said something in Japanese, which Leo interpreted as meaning "let her go," even though it was in some sort of rough street language that he didn't completely understand. The two other gangsters released Bobby's arms, and she staggered forward into Leo's arms. He hugged her tight, and he could feel her shivering.

"What the fuck's going on?" she asked. Her voice was very faint.

"I don't know. Come on, I want to look at your hand."

"It's all right. It's just a cut. Hurts, though."

"And there's a lot of blood. I'll just wrap it up for you." He pulled a handkerchief out of his pocket, and she started to giggle, almost hysterically, it seemed to him. "What's so funny?"

"You, having a handkerchief in your pocket. No-one has handkerchiefs these days. You're so sweet." She winced as he gingerly tied the cloth round her hand.

"We'll get that looked at as soon as possible," he told her, and then looked over to where Pig was still standing facing the group. His sheer bulk appeared menacing. There was almost complete silence, except for the noise of an ambulance siren somewhere in the distance.

"You killed the boss in Tokyo, didn't you?" the leader who had just slashed Bobby said to Pig. "And you know what that means."

Pig said nothing, but simply grinned and shrugged.

"You die, big man."

"Wait," said Leo. Everyone turned to look at him. "How do you know it was the Rabbits? It might have been another gang."

"You left witnesses alive," said the gangster. "A stupid thing to do."

"That means they're going to kill us, anyway," Bobby said to Leo. "After they get rid of Pig."

"She's right, I'm afraid," said the leader. "It would be most inconvenient for us if you were to tell the police about the things we're about to do. Don't think you can run away, by the way. You really wouldn't get very far. The question is, who do we start with?"

"I think I'm going to start with you," said Pig. He stepped forward, the stick, which Leo could now see was a length of heavy metal piping, probably from a lighting truss or stage scaffolding, swinging easily from his hand. "One at a time, or all together?"

"You sold us out," said the gangster. "We had an arrangement, and you broke it."

What the hell was that meant to mean? Leo asked himself. How did Pig come to have an arrangement with the yakuza in the first place? And what sort of arrangement would it be?

«What the fuck?» Bobby thought to him, echoing his thoughts.

«I don't know,» he thought back.

The three gangsters seemed unwilling to make any kind of move. Pig was in some sort of martial arts stance which made him look even more menacing. Leo had no doubt that Pig could take on two of the thugs at once, but three?

The leader transferred his knife to his left hand, and pulled something out of his pocket with his right.

"It's a gun," Bobby breathed, horrified.

"No," Leo said. He had a better view of the object. "It's a taser – one of those electric stun guns."

«Listen, Bobby,» he thought at her. «Just nod your head if you can still hear me.» To his relief, she nodded. «I think we can get the leader while his back's turned.

You take the left side, I'll take the right. You think you can manage that?» Again, she nodded.

«I've got you pretty well trained at this sending business», she thought to him, and he got the sensation of a smile from her.

«All right,» he thought, and blew a mental kiss in her direction. «Can we move a bit closer towards him?» As unobtrusively as possible, they took a few steps towards the leader. None of the gang seemed to have noticed.

«On three. I won't say it, just think it,» he thought to her. «You take left, I take right. Ready?»

She nodded.

«One, two, three,» he thought.

They moved fast, but it seemed that Bobby had temporarily forgotten her wounded hand, and withdrew with a cry of pain when she grabbed for her opponent's arm. The gangster, in his turn, wriggled easily from Leo's grip, and brought the stun-gun round, pressing it against Bobby's neck. There was a crackle, and a spark, and Bobby slumped to the floor.

The leader turned towards Leo, but was halted by the crunch of Pig's pipe into his ribcage. Leo heard a distinct crack as something broke inside, and the stun-gun dropped from the yakuza's hand.

The other two thugs, Leo now noticed, were lying on the ground, moaning. Pig had obviously already moved fast while Leo and Bobby were trying to restrain the leader.

Pig stooped fast to retrieve the stun-gun and used it on the leader, who twitched and fell to the ground beside Bobby.

"There, that's taken care of them. I'll just look after the other—" Pig broke off. A knife, thrown by one of the other gangsters, who was now propped up on one elbow, had embedded itself in his body. "Shit!" With a grimace, he started to remove the blade, and then stopped. "Not sure that the little bastard hasn't hit a vein or an artery or something inside me." He moved to his attacker, and applied the stun-gun. Another crackle, spark, twitch, and a slumped unconscious body. "Might as well make sure with the other one." He moved, seemingly in some pain from his wound, to the third thug, and repeated the process before placing the stun-gun in the man's pocket, and standing up.

"OK," he said to Leo. "Get this trash outside. We don't want it left here."

"Me?"

"Yes, you. I'm fucked. Drag these pieces of shit out into the alley at the back."

"And you can take care of Bobby?"

"I just about can manage that, I think. Just that I can't manage three of them. Get on with it."

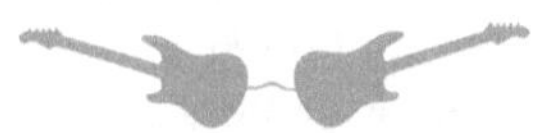

Chapter 18

I t took Leo some time to get the three bodies outside the back door of the hall, and when he had finished, Pig was standing, leaning against a stack of speakers. Bobby was nowhere to be seen.

"What have you done with her?" Leo asked.

"She's in her dressing room. She'll be fine. Don't worry about her," Pig said. "I made sure that she's in recovery position and all that. She'll wake up feeling stiff and sore with you standing beside her, taking care of her."

"He's telling the truth for once," came a familiar voice from the shadows.

"You pain me, Nick," said Pig. "I usually tell the truth."

"Except when you don't," said Nick, stepping onto the stage. He appeared to be exhausted. "It's all right, Leo. I met Pig just now coming down the corridor, dripping blood, and carrying Bobby. Or rather, trying to carry her. So, being the detective type that I am, my suspicions were a little aroused by this."

"So I told Nick what had happened."

"But not the why of it," said Nick. "Just the what."

"You're not going to kill me or attack me, are you?" Leo asked Pig. "I don't even know which bloody side you're on, do I?"

"Oh, for fuck's sake," said Pig. He dropped the pipe, throwing it over towards Leo, who bent and picked it up. "That knife cut is fucking killing me. Probably literally. I wouldn't put it past those bastards to use poison."

A chill ran through Leo when he heard the last word. "Bobby? Is she okay? What if she's been poisoned too?"

It was Nick who answered. "If she has, Leo," he said in a gentle voice, "then it's much less than Pig here. I looked at her finger after Pig told me what had happened. There's a lot of blood, but it's not a serious wound. I am pretty certain that she hasn't been poisoned."

"He's right there, I'm sure. Look at me," said Pig. "I'm sweating bullets, I puked up when I'd taken Bobby to her room, I feel like shit. She was sleeping like a baby. In any case, my little bastard was trying to kill me. Hers was only trying to hurt her, not to kill her. She'd have been useless as a hostage if she died. Think about it."

Leo did think about it, and felt a little better. "Even so," he said, but Pig held up a warning finger.

"Shut up and ask me questions, why don't you, while you still have the chance? I've got this feeling that it's not going to be that long now."

"Okay." Leo looked at Pig. "So you were the one buggering things up, weren't you? I was pretty certain it was you. Did you know that I knew?"

"How did you work that out? The famous Leo's luck?" Nick asked. "I remember when I first met you, you looked like shit. Remember? You'd just run out on your wife, and your bit on the side—"

"Don't go on."

"I wasn't going to make a thing of it. But I remember that even though you really needed help, I could tell you were something special."

"Me, special?"

"Yeah, you know you are. You're the first person Bobby's really been able to relate to since— Never mind since when. You've got these talents, and you're lucky."

"I saw that when you brought him in," said Pig. "Nick doesn't usually fuck up when he finds people, and I was pretty sure he hadn't fucked up with you." Pig was sweating now, and his face was pale, but he still looked as though he could destroy Leo with one sweep of his arm. "Anyway, was it your luck that told you it was me?"

"Not that. Remember, I look for patterns. Patterns in money. I still have ways of finding out how money moves, and where it comes from and where it goes to."

"He told Bobby and me that's what he was going to do," said Nick. "Didn't he tell you at the same time? In Tokyo or after that?"

Pig shook his head.

"You called it a 'goldseam', remember, when you told me how you were being ripped off?" said Leo. "I'm pretty good at it, you know. Better than your Rabbits."

Pig looked stunned. "You hacked my bank accounts? Including the one in the Channel Islands?"

"And the one in Luxembourg."

Pig raised his eyebrows. "You are pretty good at this, aren't you?"

"Didn't realise you had any kind of side deal going with these guys, though." Leo indicated the fallen gangsters. "And of course, there's always the big question. Why?"

Pig laughed bitterly. "Why? How long have you got? How many reasons do you want?" He paused. "Look, I'm not about to fucking hurt you. You've won and I've lost. I'm a good loser. And I am a loser, believe me. This fucking thing hurts more than it should, given that it wasn't that deep or anything. I'm pretty sure that these fuckers would use a poisoned knife, so then there'll be nothing anyone can do for me. Drop that pipe, and relax."

Reluctantly, Leo abandoned the pipe and let it fall to the ground. Despite everything he had learned in the past minutes, and what he suspected, he still trusted Pig.

"Thanks." Surprising tears started to flow down the big man's face, running into his beard, and losing themselves there. "I told you I knew Nick and Bobby from kids, right? I loved Bobby as I watched her grow up. I mean, I really loved her. I wanted to marry her. She knew that. You knew that, Nick, didn't you?"

The guitarist nodded. "I did, and I know why she didn't want to marry you. She told me after it had happened and it was all over. You never knew I knew, did you, Pig?"

"Shit, no. And you still kept me as your friend. Jesus, Nick, you're a good man." He advanced on Nick, his arms outstretched, and surprisingly, hugged the smaller man, his body heaving with sobs. "Thank you. God, I never knew you knew. Thank you." There was silence, broken only by the sound of Pig's breathing. Eventually, Pig broke the embrace, and stood back, seemingly more self-composed.

"What happened?" Leo asked, sensing that the time was now ready for him to ask questions once more.

"Shall I tell him, or are you up to it?" Nick asked Pig,

who stood in silence for what seemed like an age before answering him.

"I'll tell him," Pig said slowly. "I'm the one who fucked things up, after all. She told me she couldn't marry me. She said to me that she liked me as a friend, but there was no way that she could ever marry a murderer. Fuck." Pig winced. "This fucking knife. What a way to go." He grimaced, and with a violent wrench, pulled out the knife. He gasped, and seemed unable to speak for at least a minute. Leo waited in silence while the big man sucked in air greedily. "It burns, you know." He pointed to the place where the knife had entered. "And then it goes numb. And it's spreading. What a way to go," he repeated. He dropped the knife into his pocket.

"What did she mean by calling you a murderer?" Leo asked when Pig seemed a little more in control of himself.

"Okay. You know I have all these fancy letters after my name? They're real enough, sure, but while I was studying to get them, I was leading a double life. I was leading a biker gang at night, and being a good little post-grad student in the day time. And we were ripping off little corner stores, getting into fights with other gangs for no good reason. Viking stuff, like. Bit of looting, pillaging…"

"And raping?"

Pig shook his head. "No. I never tolerated that sort of shit. Maybe I saw every woman as the sister I never had, or as Bobby, the woman in my life."

"I knew that much about him," said Nick. "Maybe that's why I wasn't going to cut you loose as a friend. You had principles."

"Fuck principles," replied Pig. "I lost them that one

time. One of the bikers got tired of us or something. Talked to the police, and three of my mates got sent down for a couple of years. He didn't have enough shit on me to get me sent down, but it was a close thing. When we found out who the bastard was who'd set us up, I decided to teach him a lesson that the others would never forget. Took him out into a field in the middle of the countryside one night, staked him out on the ground, poured petrol over him, and tossed a match onto him. He screamed." Pig paused and wiped his forehead. "I can hear those screams even now."

"This was you or the gang did this? Why are you blaming yourself?" asked Leo.

"I had help with it, sure. But it was my idea. I poured the petrol. I tossed the match. I killed that poor bastard. If it had been the others who'd done it, I could have stopped them, I guess. But I know I sure as hell wouldn't have done."

"And Bobby found out about this?"

"I was drunk. I was drunk all the time after that. I was drinking a bottle of whisky a day to forget what I'd done. I knew that night that I'd really fucked up the rest of my life. The guy's first scream was enough to tell me that. And Bobby asked me what was wrong one evening when I was out of my head and going round feeling sorry for myself." Pig was sweating freely by now. "Jesus Christ, I feel fucking terrible."

"And?" Leo wasn't going to let up.

"What do you think? I told her what I'd done, and she threw up. Literally. She threw up. And then she told me that there was no way she could ever consider herself in love with me ever again. She was prepared to continue being my friend for old times' sake, but as for anything else, let alone marriage, forget it. And that really hurt, believe me."

Leo said nothing, but continued looking at the enormous long-haired biker, who appeared to be on the verge of unlikely tears once more. He looked over at Nick, but Nick was studiously looking away. He guessed that this was dredging up painful memories for him as well as for Pig.

"After that, I still loved her. I mean I adored her. I worshipped the ground she trod on. And I hated her at the same time. Can you understand that?" Leo nodded. "Good for you, mate, because I couldn't, and I still can't. I couldn't bear to let her out of my sight, but I couldn't stand being in the same room as her sometimes. Crazy, eh?"

"And then you came up with this idea, Nick. Using your talent to get money, and she was against it?" Leo prompted.

Nick nodded, but Pig answered.

"Yeah, what I told you on the plane that time was true. Money isn't everything, sure, but Bobby's attitude was going to screw us every which way if she refused to play with us. That didn't help matters between her and me, either. Of course Nick wasn't going to argue with his little sister, was he?"

"I certainly wasn't. She's got a temper when she's roused," said Nick, smiling thinly.

"And I couldn't argue with both of them, so Bobby got what she wanted."

"But you didn't want?"

"I felt we were wasting talent there – not to mention money. And I'd developed an expensive habit."

"I thought you didn't do drugs."

"I don't. I did casinos. Remember all the lucky Rabbits? Well, I'm the unlucky Rabbit. I don't win a damn thing in casinos, and it took me quite a lot of money and quite a lot of time to discover that my bad luck is as consistent as the other Rabbits' luck is good. I was way down in the hole. The Rabbit hole if you like."

"So you sold out?"

"You're hurting me, Leo, by using those words. I never sold out. I just saw a way in which I could use Nick's and Bobby's talent and the Rabbits to help me out of trouble."

"What sort of trouble, Pig? Why couldn't you have come to us? Bobby and I would have helped you, you know that." Nick appeared concerned.

Pig shook his head. "Pride, mate. Stupid bloody pride. Those guys in Vegas. Maybe it's not the Mob running things there any more, but it might as well be, the way they talked to me. I was going to be a dead man unless I could come up with a couple of hundred grand. For starters, that is."

Leo whistled. "That much?"

"Yeah, that much. So what I did was to make contact through Yamagami Senior. I had sort of guessed that the company was in bed with the wrong people, but they were the only ones who claimed to know the right people to make the Feelers, and they did a good job of it first time round."

"How do you mean, 'first time'?"

"For the first year or so we were working this thing, the Feelers were strictly on the level. What Nick and Bobby got from the audience went to the Feelers, and the Feelers passed on straight data to the computers. The customers got what they wanted – accurate data, and it got more accurate as time went on and we got better at things. Worked a treat, didn't it, Nick?"

"Sure did, Pig."

"But then I arranged with Yamagami to make me some duplicate ones with a couple of gimmicks which allowed me to switch them over to produce the results I wanted when I wanted them."

"And so you were selling these faked results to the highest bidders?"

"Sort of. Not quite. I didn't think all that peace shit was going to do anything. Sure, save the whales, fight nuclear energy, whatever. All good stuff, right? But this peace stuff? Who's going to fight the military-industrial complex and come out a winner, eh?"

"It happens," Nick said, a little doggedly. "You stupid bastard, Pig. You should have talked to us. We'd have helped you."

"You don't win against them nearly as often as you think, Nick. I did my sums. Even if the Rabbits were supplying one hundred percent accurate data, I didn't see that anyone was ever going to win against that lot. But I contacted these bastards, to make sure that the other side – the good guys – never got the truth delivered to them. They then paid me to make sure that the Rabbits didn't deliver anything worth delivering to the other side."

"But the Rabbits lost money over that. How could you square that one?" asked Leo.

"Correction. They didn't lose money. They didn't make money. I made sure the contracts said that there were no legal comebacks if the Rabbits failed to deliver. After all, we're talking telepathy here, aren't we? How the hell can you put that into a legal contract?"

Leo considered what Pig had just told him. "You cleared your Vegas debts?"

"Oh yes, very quickly indeed. They paid me as agreed. And I wanted to stop. Don't imagine I felt good – feel good about all this. I'm a world-class shit, you know. With a conscience. But once you've started on something like this, you can't let go of the tiger's tail. Do I have to go on?"

"Except for that last time with Yamagami, the Rabbits didn't lose money. Yamagami claimed damages, didn't they?" asked Nick, in a somewhat sharper tone than he had been using up to then. "What the fuck was going on there?"

Pig sighed. "Yeah. Look, my arm is fucking killing me. I'm not going anywhere. Mind if I sit down?" Without waiting for their permission, he lowered himself to the ground, wincing as his arm touched the floor. "I've fucking had it, you bastards," he said, seemingly to the absent gangsters, but without anger. "Yeah, Yamagami," he said, reflectively. "That little prick slipped that clause in behind my back. And he was taking some of my cut as well as soon as he found out what I was up to. And he made passes at Bobby once he'd worked out she was a girl. Never got anywhere with her, but I had to pull him off her once. That didn't make me a friend of his."

"You didn't tell me about any of this." Nick sounded accusing.

"No way. Yamagami had me by the balls. I tell you about the clause, Yamagami shops me to you and Bobby and the rest of the Rabbits, and then where am I? Mexican standoff."

Leo nodded.

Pig continued. "So then Yamagami asks for something which wasn't on the radar – that was his mistake, not asking about the love and peace and all the rest of it, because that really stood out like a sore prick, and then the results got buggered up."

"How did he manage to do that?"

"He didn't." Pig smiled, and then coughed. "I wasn't going to let the bastard have the answers. He didn't deserve them. That's what really pissed him off. I'd been itching to get my own back on him for some time. And I only spotted that non-performance clause after we'd played the gigs. I kicked myself hard over missing that. So then, what happened in Tokyo the other day was justice, and no more than he deserved, believe me. Father's no better. Up to his eyeballs in the yakuza, as you spotted very quickly, and he's not going to call the cops in a hurry, for sure. I doubt if the yakuza will be too happy with him, either. His son's death may call too much attention to them from the police for comfort."

"It sounds as though you've told me most of it, except the technical bits. How it works."

Pig laughed, and immediately started to cough again. "You don't need to know that. It's not interesting. All you need to know is that it does work, and what it does. The rest really isn't relevant. Look, Nick, I'm sorry, you know that, mate."

"I know it, Pig." There were tears in Nick's eyes. "But the end is here."

"The end is right here. I've come to the end, haven't I?" asked Pig.

"You have, old friend." This time it was Nick who went up to the big biker and embraced him.

"We've had some good times, mate," said Pig.

"That's how I'll remember you," said Nick. "The good times. I'll forget all this stupid shit."

"You're a good man, Nick. A good man," Pig repeated. "And Bobby's bloody fantastic. Give her a kiss from me, will you?" It wasn't sure whether he was talking to Nick or Leo, as he bent over and retched while saying those last words.

"You're going to die, aren't you?" To his own surprise, Leo seemed detached about the whole business.

"Looks like it, doesn't it? I suppose I'd better go somewhere else to do it. Could lead to some awkward questions, I suppose, if I'm left lying about the place like this."

"What do you mean?" asked Nick

"You'll never see me again." Pig tried to rise to his feet and groaned. "Help me up, will you? It will take both of you." Nick and Leo helped the big man to stand up, one on each side of him. "Give me that pipe. I need something to lean on." Wordlessly, Leo passed it to him, and he hobbled to the back of the stage, leaning heavily on the pipe and wheezing loudly. "You're a lucky fucker. Hope you know just how lucky you are." He opened the stage door. "Canal's down this way, isn't it? That's where I'm going."

With a shock, Leo realised what Pig meant. "You can't do that," he said. "There's got to be something someone can do for you."

"Can and will do it," said Pig. "This fucking shit is getting to me. Too late for anyone to do anything." He moved, slowly and obviously in pain, in the direction of the canal.

"Let him do it," said Nick. "This is the end for him."

"Wait!" Leo called after him.

Pig slowly turned his head.

"What's your name?" Leo left the building and walked towards Pig.

"Pig. You know that. Now piss off and leave me alone. Go and look after Bobby or something."

"No, the name you had before you were Pig."

"Don't laugh."

"I won't. Promise."

"I'm only telling you this because you'll never see me alive again, you understand? You tell anyone else, and I swear I will come back and haunt the shit out of you. Cedric. Cedric Lionel Tomlinson-Smythe, if you really want it in its full horrible glory."

"Pig's better, isn't it? I see that."

Pig nodded and paused. "Here." He rummaged in his pocket, and held something out towards Leo, resting on the palm of his hand. "Take it."

Leo approached, and saw a pink plastic pig. He picked it up out of Pig's hand.

"It's your badge of honour. Keep it in your beer at all times," said Pig. "I'm handing over to you. You're the new Pig, you know, Leo. Let your hair grow, grow yourself a beard, if Bobby will let you. Drink a bit more, get a gut on you. They'll forget me, and you'll be the stuff of legend." He turned. "Goodbye and good luck," said Cedric. He turned away, and limped into the darkness.

"Goodbye," said the new Pig. There wasn't anything else left to say. As he turned back to face Nick, who was still standing in the doorway, he heard a voice in his head.

«What's happening? Where are you? I love you.»

«I'll be with you in a moment. Darling.»

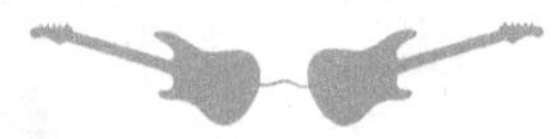

If you enjoyed this book...

Thank you for reading this story – I hope you enjoyed it.

It would be highly appreciated if you left a review or rating on one of the usual outlets.

You may also enjoy some of my other books, which are available from the usual outlets.

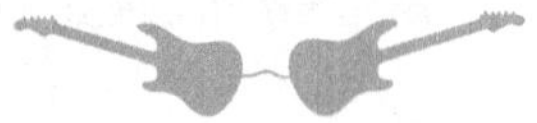

Also by Hugh Ashton

All titles in both paper and ebook format unless otherwise noted.

Sherlock Holmes Titles

Tales from the Deed Box of John H. Watson M.D.

More from the Deed Box of John H. Watson M.D.

Secrets from the Deed Box of John H. Watson M.D.

The Darlington Substitution

*The Case of the Trepoff Murder**

Notes from the Dispatch-Box of John H. Watson M.D.

Further Notes from the Dispatch-Box of John H. Watson M.D.

The Death of Cardinal Tosca

The Last Notes from the Dispatch-Box of John H. Watson M.D.

1894

Without My Boswell

The Lichfield Murder†

Some Singular Cases of Mr. Sherlock Holmes

*The Adventure of Vanaprastha**

*   ebook only
†   paper only

Tales of Old Japanese
*The Untime**
*The Untime Revisited**
The Untime & The Untime Revisited[†]
Balance of Powers
Angels Unawares
Beneath Gray Skies
Red Wheels Turning
At the Sharpe End
*The Persian Dagger (with M.Lowe)**

Sherlock Ferret and the Missing Necklace[†]
Sherlock Ferret and the Multiplying Masterpieces[†]
Sherlock Ferret and the Poisoned Pond[†]
Sherlock Ferret and the Phantom Photographer[†]
The Adventures of Sherlock Ferret[†]

About the Author

Hugh Ashton was born in the United Kingdom, and moved to Japan in 1988, where he lived until his return to the UK in 2016.

He is best known for his Sherlock Holmes stories, which have been hailed as some of the most authentic pastiches on the market, and have received favourable reviews from Sherlockians and non-Sherlockians alike.

He currently lives in the historic city of Lichfield with his wife, Yoshiko.

His ramblings may be found on Facebook, Twitter, and in various other places on the Internet. He may be contacted at: author@HughAshtonBooks.com